Playing detective.

We trailed Ginger past Lauren's turnoff on Brio Drive, and Ginger still kept going, past Lenox Road, Birchwood Circle, and Eagle Lane.

By now, I was definitely getting tired of playing detective. I was just going to say so to Lauren when Ginger made a sharp left turn. I was so surprised that I almost tipped over! Lauren was, too.

"Ginger's turning onto Mill Road!" she cried, screeching to a stop on the shoulder. Mill Road is Patti's street. "Come on," Lauren said.

We zoomed across Hillcrest and up Mill Road until we were almost even with the Jenkinses' driveway. Then we got off our bikes, pushed them into the hedge, and crawled in ourselves to peer out at Patti's house from between the branches.

"She's here!" Lauren said. "That's Ginger's bike beside the front steps! I can't believe it! Patti is Ginger's next victim!"

Look for these and other books
in the Sleepover Friends Series:

Lauren's Afterschool Job

Susan Saunders

AN
APPLE
PAPERBACK

SCHOLASTIC INC.
New York Toronto London Auckland Sydney

ISBN 0-590-43928-6

Copyright © 1990 by Daniel Weiss Associates, Inc. All rights reserved. Published by Scholastic Inc. APPLE PAPERBACKS is a registered trademark of Scholastic Inc. SLEEPOVER FRIENDS is a registered trademark of Daniel Weiss Associates, Inc.

12 11 10 9 8 7 6 5 4 3 2 1   0 1 2 3 4 5/9

Printed in the U.S.A.   28

First Scholastic printing, December 1990

Chapter
1

"I think I'm getting too old for bunk beds," Lauren Hunter said, frowning at the two tired wooden bunks pushed into a corner of her new bedroom. "And I *know* I'm getting too tall — Patti and I practically hang over the ends of these already!"

Patti Jenkins nodded in agreement. She and Lauren are the tallest girls in our fifth-grade class at Riverhurst Elementary.

"Plus, the bunks looked fine in your old room on Pine Street, but they kind of get lost here on Brio Drive," Kate Beekman said, studying the big, airy space painted a nice French vanilla color.

Kate scooted Lauren's cat Rocky out of the way and plopped down on the bottom bunk. "So what kind of beds do you want, Lauren? Twins, or a double bed?"

"Or maybe pullout couches, like the ones I've got. Red-black-and-white ones would look great in here!" I suggested. I'm Stephanie Green. I realize that Lauren's usually the one who brings you up-to-date on the four of us. But lately she's been so distracted by the move and everything . . . I volunteered to help out!

Just a short while ago, Lauren's family left the house they've always lived in on Pine Street for a much bigger, older, and more . . . uh . . . *unusual* house on Brio Drive. (Though still in Riverhurst, thank goodness!) Finally, Lauren's beginning to think the new house has lots of interesting possibilities.

For example, it's huge, it has three real fireplaces, and it even has a funny, tiny, old-fashioned elevator called a dumbwaiter that you can climb into and ride up and down between floors with sleepover snacks. Plus, it's got a neat little deck on the roof that's great for keeping an eye on Willie Judd, the cutest boy in sixth grade — he lives right down the block.

When Lauren first moved in, though, she thought the house was about as appealing as "Nightmare Mansion" on "Friday Night Chillers" on Channel 21. You know the one — that creaky old three-story ruin at the beginning of every program, with cracked windowpanes in all the windows, a front door hanging off its hinges, and ghosts oozing out of the chimneys!

"There are other colors besides red, black, and white, Stephanie," Kate was saying firmly. Which, of course, I know. It's just that red, black, and white goes with practically everything, looks so cool, and coincidentally, just happens to be my favorite color combination. So sue me!

"Besides, my family sure can't afford to rush out and buy new pullout couches right now. With Dad starting his own real estate business, our old house not sold yet, the humongous hole in the living-room floor here to take care of, the bathroom pipes to fix, and five whole windows to replace, at least. . . ." Lauren said glumly.

I didn't really know what to say to cheer her up. New furniture *is* expensive! I mean, my parents just bought a new chest of drawers for Emma and Jeremy, my baby brother and sister, so I knew.

"Lauren, I have a great idea — Dad just got a new bed for the spare bedroom," Patti said. "So I know beds don't have to cost a lot of money. My dad found this bed at a place where some of the university students go to buy secondhand furniture."

Mr. and Mrs. Jenkins are both history professors at the university here.

"Secondhand?" Lauren said doubtfully. "Other people's old junk?"

"It's not all junk. Dad's going to pick up an end table there, too," Patti said.

"And secondhand clothes can be great, so why not secondhand furniture?" I said. "Think of the terrific stuff at Clothing Classics!" Clothing Classics sells fabulous old clothes at rock-bottom prices.

"Like that tie-dyed red-and-black T-shirt I bought for a dollar," I continued. Tie-dyes are really in again. "And the bell-bottoms with the paisley patches on them only cost seventy-five cents, and — "

"If you start listing all the stuff you've carted away from Clothing Classics, the sun will set before you're finished!" Kate interrupted. "And we won't have time to check out the furniture store!"

"You mean we'll go right now?" Lauren said, brightening up a little.

"Why not?" I said. "We've got a couple of hours before dinner." Since her mom started working full time, Lauren often gets dinner started.

"Where is this place, Patti?" Kate asked as the four of us pulled on our jackets — I was wearing my black leather jacket with red trim — and raced down the Hunters' back stairs.

"Out on the Loop," Patti said. "On the way to

4

Tully's Fish Market. You know the little wooden shops all in a row there? It's one of those. It's called Alice's Attic."

"Make sure the gate's closed," Lauren warned as we headed down the brick sidewalk toward the garage. "Bullwinkle's run off twice in the last week, and it takes forever to catch him."

Bullwinkle is the Hunters' enormous black dog, who's about the size of a baby elephant and twice as rambunctious.

But Bullwinkle didn't look very serious about making an escape that afternoon. He was lying on his side in the sun and he barely raised his head when we walked past him — thank goodness! When Bullwinkle is feeling friendly, he drools so much it's like stepping into a warm shower!

When Lauren's brother Roger first picked Bullwinkle out, he was a teeny, furry, black puppy. The people at the animal shelter thought he was part cocker spaniel. It turned out he was part *Newfoundland,* and that teeny little puppy now weighs almost as much as me and Lauren put together! He's a real sweetheart, though, and his fur *is* a nice color. I think I'll have to buy him a *red* collar. . . .

Anyway, we locked the gate behind us, grabbed our bikes, and pedaled down Brio Drive toward Hillcrest. To the right, Hillcrest runs south to Main Street, past Patti's street, Mill Road, and Pine Street.

Pine Street is where Kate and I live, and Lauren, too, until last month. Her house was practically next door to Kate's — there was only one house in between them. So Lauren and Kate started playing together when they were in diapers. By the time they were in kindergarten, they were best friends, and that's when the sleepovers started. It got to be such a habit that Dr. Beekman, Kate's dad, started calling them the Sleepover Twins.

Not that there's anything even vaguely twinlike about them. As I mentioned, Lauren is tall. She's also thin — she can eat like a pig and never gain an ounce, the lucky thing. She has brown hair that hangs straight to her shoulders, fair skin, and hazel eyes.

Kate is short, and she has blonde hair that comes just about to the bottom of her neck. She brushes it back from her face on the sides and top. Kate has green eyes with little brown flecks in them, and she wears glasses sometimes — she's kind of nearsighted.

Kate and Lauren don't act alike any more than they look alike. Lauren is easygoing and a little messy. She's also sort of a jock. She does okay in school, too, except for math, where she does a lot better than okay — she's as good at math as she is at baseball, which is to say *excellent*!

Kate is super-neat, super-organized, and not at all into sports, except maybe as a manager. She's serious about studying and making good grades. But what she's really nuts about are movies, any kind of movie, including those foreign ones where you have to read the words at the bottom of the screen to find out what's going on. And she has strong opinions about practically everything. So if you don't happen to agree with her . . . let's just say that Kate and I had some problems in the beginning, because I have some pretty strong opinions myself!

I arrived on the scene in Riverhurst the summer before fourth grade. My dad's a lawyer, and he was offered a really good job here, at Blake, Binder, and Rosten. So he and my mom and I packed up everything we owned, left our city apartment behind, and moved into a house at the far end of Pine Street.

I was pretty sad to leave the city — I mean, I grew up there — and all my friends, my school, even my grandmother, Nana Bricker. (I guess you know she's Nana Kessler now.) It wasn't easy starting over again in a strange town. Even now, I can't say that I would definitely choose Riverhurst over the city — but one thing's for sure: The only way I could move back is if I took the Sleepover Friends with me!

I met Lauren first — she and I were both in 4A, Mr. Civello's class. We hit it off right away. Part of it was that Lauren gets along with almost everybody. But we also thought the same things were funny, like Henry Larkin, a boy in our class, pretending to be in love with Jenny Carlin, a girl in our class who can't stand him. And Lauren and I like the same rock groups — Heat and the Jangles. We both love hanging out at the mall on Saturdays. I felt as though we'd been friends forever. So when Lauren introduced me to Kate Beekman, *her* best friend, I just knew Kate and I would be instant friends, too.

Wro-ong! I've never been so off base — except maybe when I decided that vests were out this year. . . .

Anyway, Lauren asked me to a Friday sleepover at her house with Kate. The first thing Kate did was announce that we couldn't watch "Battle of the British Bands" on *Video Trax* because there was some forty-year-old Lithuanian movie, or something like that, on at the same time, and she absolutely *had* to see it. And I'd been waiting for months to see "Battle of the British Bands"!! I'd never heard of anything so pushy in all my life!

The sleepover went downhill from there. Kate and I argued about absolutely everything, from clothes to the weather. In fact, by Saturday morning, it was crystal clear that Kate and I agreed on one thing only — neither of us wanted to spend another second together if we could possibly help it! I thought Kate took herself so seriously that she ended up being a total drag. And I guess she thought I was a complete ditz who gabbed on and on about rock stars and shopping.

But I guess Lauren could see some hope beneath the surface disagreements. Anyway, she didn't give up. After a couple more of Lauren's clever plans to get us together, Kate and I could actually stand to be in the same room. And little by little, the Sleepover Twins became the Sleepover Trio.

I got to know the good things about Kate, like her loyalty, and how sensible and helpful she is when the chips are down. She can be funny, too, and whether we're planning a party or a picnic, or just a trip to the mall, she's the best organizer there is. Still, we didn't always see eye to eye. I think some-times Lauren felt she was walking a tightrope be-tween us! So when Patti showed up this year in Mrs. Mead's class with the three of us, I couldn't have been happier to see her!

Patti's from the city, too — we had even gone to the same school in kindergarten and first grade. Patti's one of the nicest people you'd ever want to meet, and one of the smartest, too. She probably has the highest grades at Riverhurst Elementary. Plus, she's good at sports. Patti's quiet and sort of shy, but she's the best kind of friend, somebody you know you can always count on, no matter what. And she's even taller than Lauren, which makes Lauren happy. She wasn't enjoying being the tallest girl in the fifth grade.

Lauren and Kate liked Patti right away, of course. School had hardly started this fall and suddenly there were *four* Sleepover Friends! We've been through a lot together in the last few months — like when Patti almost moved to Alaska. And when my baby brother and sister were born, ending my brilliant career as an only child. And when Kate had problems with a certain boy. And when Lauren moved away from the house she's always lived in on Pine Street . . .

"Hey, come on, you guys!" Lauren called over her shoulder. She was turning left on Hillcrest toward the Loop. Lauren and Patti have such long legs that Kate and I have to pedal like crazy to keep up!

I was panting like crazy by the time we coasted into the parking lot. And thirsty! I was absolutely dying for a chocolate shake! I know, I know — there are about three hundred calories in a chocolate shake. But I figured I'd used up *five* hundred calories at least, just getting there!

Chapter 2

I was disappointed to see there weren't any ice-cream shops in the row. There was a dry cleaner's, a tanning salon called Tanfastic, and a brand-new Video Connection, where you can rent all the latest movies (the Video Connection on East Main is one of Kate's favorite places). At the very end was a building that looked like a small red barn. Two bay windows stuck out of it, one on each end, and two doors were set side-by-side in the center; one door was green, the other bright yellow.

"Is that it?" Kate asked Patti as we carefully steered around parked cars.

"It must be — Dad mentioned that it was in sort of a barn," Patti answered, braking her bike at the curb.

Lauren, Kate, and I rolled up beside her. " 'Alice's Attic,' " Lauren read the gold script on the plate-glass window. " 'Alice McWhinny, Prop.' What's a 'Prop.'?"

"Short for *proprietor*," Patti explained. "It just means 'owner.' " Sometimes I wonder if there's anything that Patti doesn't know!

As we leaned our bikes against a wooden flower planter out front, Kate suddenly hissed, "Heads up — it's Ginger Kinkaid!"

"Where?!" Lauren said, her head swiveling around like one of those radar dishes.

"She's coming out of the yellow door!" Kate said. "Quick — in here!" She dashed into the Video Connection with the three of us right behind her.

"Why are we hiding?" I asked.

"I for one don't feel like talking to Ginger today. Anyway, what's *she* doing here?" Lauren muttered as we crouched down behind an open rack of videocassettes.

"Well, it *is* a mini-mall. Maybe she's shopping," Patti giggled.

Lauren rolled her eyes at Patti. "Ginger wouldn't be caught dead shopping at one of these secondhand places."

"No way," I agreed. Ginger is about the biggest snob in the world. She'll only shop in the fanciest stores — no Clothing Classics for her — and wears only designer labels.

"Who cares *why* she's here?" Lauren grumbled. "It's bound to be bad luck for me!"

"Ginger is bad luck for all of us," Kate reminded her.

Ginger is a fifth-grader, like the four of us, only she's in 5C, Mr. Patterson's class. She's pretty new at Riverhurst Elementary — she's only been here for a few months. She's lived in lots of different places because her dad was a captain in the Air Force. But being new didn't seem to bother her a bit. Especially around boys. She had them practically eating out of her hand her first day at school.

Ginger has a southern accent that she can turn on or off — it's mostly *on* around boys, or if she wants to impress somebody. I guess she's cute enough — she has thick, reddish-brown hair long enough for a French braid, and she's taller than I am, with round brown eyes and kind of peach-colored skin. She has pierced ears, and about a hundred pairs of earrings — I don't think I've ever seen the same ones twice. Of course, who'd want to get close enough to see?

Lauren was the first person to know her. That was because at the time, Lauren's dad was working at Blaney Realty for Mr. Blaney, who just happens to be Ginger's uncle. So Mr. Blaney introduced Ginger to Lauren.

But Ginger wasn't satisfied with just *knowing* Lauren, or being her friend. She wanted to be Lauren's *only* friend. Forget the fact that *we* were here first — Ginger tried her best to turn Lauren against Kate, Patti, and me. Then, after causing a truckload of trouble, she decided that Lauren wasn't good enough for her. So she dumped Lauren and started hanging around with Christy Soames — Christy is the biggest fashion plate at Riverhurst Elementary.

Ginger and Christy began to dress alike, wear their hair alike, talk alike, and they've been practically stitched together with invisible thread ever since.

We were actually forced to work with them a little while ago. The Sleepover Friends were putting together a float for the Homecoming parade, celebrating Riverhurst School's fiftieth birthday, or whatever you want to call it. Since Blaney Realty was sponsoring the float, we ended up having to work with Ginger and Christy.

If you think that Kate and I sometimes bump heads, you should have seen what happened when Kate and Ginger *both* wanted to be in charge! All I can say is, it was pretty nerve-racking. Fortunately, it all worked out in the end. But we're still not really friendly with Ginger or Christy, to say the least.

Now I turned my head sideways to squint between two videocassette boxes, just in time to see Ginger roll past our hideout on her bike. She was wearing what looked like a whole new outfit — a loose, royal-blue jacket with a hood and turquoise lining, and black jeans rolled up over blue leggings. I have to admit it — she has a great eye for clothes. But the weird thing was that she was alone.

"That's weird — where's her clone?" Lauren said, taking the words right out of my mouth. The four of us shot out from behind the videocassette rack to stare through the window at Ginger's retreating back.

"Christy must be sick," I said. "Or they'd be yoked together as usual."

"Do you ladies need something, or are you just playing hide-and-seek?" said the guy sitting behind the checkout counter who had lowered his newspaper just long enough to ask.

"We're just browsing," Kate replied briskly. We strolled out of the video store and over to Alice's Attic.

There were a couple of cardboard signs taped

to the dusty plate-glass window. *Part-time help wanted*, the larger sign read. And the smaller one said, *Use green door only*.

"Okay by me," Lauren said. "Since Ginger came out of the yellow door, I'd definitely go for the green one, anyway."

"Hey, the yellow door is another secondhand store," Kate pointed out. " 'Bernice's Basement. Used furniture bought and sold. Bargains, bargains, bargains!!!' " she read. "What could Ginger have been up to in there?"

I shrugged. "She probably just dropped by to feel superior about her own furniture," I said.

"Maybe she was getting rid of some old stuff to make room for new?" Patti guessed.

"Yeah — my dad says her parents buy her anything she wants, so maybe she decided to make a few dollars off her throwaways and clear the decks for new shipments," Lauren said.

"Let's check out Bernice's after we're done with Alice's," Kate said.

As it turned out, though, we never made it next door because Lauren spotted the bed of her dreams in Alice's Attic the minute we stepped inside. Well, not exactly the *minute* we stepped inside — there were so many things to look at in there that it took a while to focus on any one of them.

The walls in Alice's Attic were covered from floor to ceiling with shelves, and the shelves were stacked with everything under the sun — from old, brown mixing bowls to crumbling used books to slightly rusty tools. All the bigger items were either piled on the floor or hanging from the rafters: chairs and bureaus with the paint peeling off, rickety tables, dented metal trunks like the one I took to camp in third grade . . . a big, old, wool coat with some buttons missing.

But there was good stuff, too: a small red-and-black chest with a top that locked, four cute black-and-white metal chairs like the ones at Thompson's Ice-Cream Parlor in Dannerville, a great picture frame made entirely of wooden spools, a red floppy hat that I just *had* to try on. *And*, a truly terrific, white iron double bed with brass knobs that Lauren went absolutely bananas over!

"This is it!" she exclaimed, hurdling a coffee table to get to it. "Wow! Would this look fabulous in my room or what?!"

"Outstanding!" Patti agreed. "It reminds me of Marcy Monroe's bed on *Made for Each Other*!" That's our favorite TV program, the one on Tuesdays with Kevin DeSpain.

"I bet it's expensive," Lauren said, discouraged. She polished a brass knob longingly with the sleeve of her jacket and sighed.

"There are no tags on anything," Kate said, and sneezed. She's allergic to dust. "Where's the 'Prop.'? We need to ask how much it is." We all peered around in the gloom.

"Hellooo!" A small, stocky woman suddenly popped out from behind a blue wardrobe in the far corner and made us jump. She had short, gray hair, glasses, and an absentminded smile. Her navy-and-red sweatsuit was streaked with dirt and there was a cobweb on her shoulder. She was carrying a feather duster, but it seemed like a lost cause to me.

"Doing some cleaning," she said brightly. Then she added hopefully, "Have you come about the job? I'm Mrs. Alice McWhinny."

"The job?" Kate said, puzzled. I guess she hadn't noticed the sign in the window. "No — we were wondering how much this iron bed costs."

The woman squinted more closely at us. "You're younger than I imagined," she said vaguely.

"The iron bed?" Patti prompted her.

"Oh, yes. The iron double bed. It's one hundred dollars," Alice told us.

Lauren groaned and headed toward the door.

But Kate grabbed the back of her jacket. "Hold on a second, Lauren."

"The bed is about eighty or ninety years old," Alice added.

"Just like your house, Lauren!" Patti said. "Wasn't it built around the turn of the century?"

"And it's in very good condition." Alice flicked another cobweb off an ancient eggbeater with her feather duster. "I really do need someone to help me out a few afternoons a week. Dusting, neatening up a little . . ." Alice's mind was still very much on the business of hiring somebody to work in the shop.

At the rate of a few afternoons a week, neatening up this mess should take, oh, about ten or fifteen years, I was thinking.

"And it would be wonderful if someone could figure out sales tax and make change for the customers," Mrs. McWhinny went on wistfully.

"Lauren, maybe *you* could help her out! Just until you paid off the bed!" Kate whispered suddenly.

"Me?" Lauren asked, startled.

"Why not?" Patti murmured, taking up the idea. "Your math couldn't be better, you can figure out totals in your head like a computer. . . ."

"I don't know if Mom and Dad would let me," Lauren said doubtfully. She lowered her voice. "Plus,

19

it would get sort of lonesome without you guys, don't you think?'' She nodded in Alice's direction.

I knew that Kate and Patti didn't have any free time, because Kate's really busy with the Video Club, and Patti's working on a complicated project for the Quarks, a club for elementary-school kids who are science whizzes. But maybe *I* could keep Lauren company, at least in the beginning!

I'd just spotted a darling old rocking horse — actually, a rocking zebra, with a little red saddle. Emma and Jeremy would love it, when they got old enough. How can you miss with red, black, and white?!

"Maybe I could work toward that zebra for the twins, Lauren, while you work toward the bed!" I said.

"Would you, Stephanie?" Lauren said, excited.

"I'll have to talk to my parents," I said. But I was pretty sure they'd go for it. They're always saying how important it is for kids to learn the value of a dollar.

"Would you consider hiring *two* people?" Kate was asking Alice McWhinny. "And instead of paying them, let them work toward a couple of things from your store?"

"That might turn out nicely," Alice said. "But

what about school? You *are* in school, aren't you?'' Yes, Alice was a little out of touch. I mean, we're only eleven! We haven't exactly had time to graduate!

"School's over at three," Lauren explained. "We can get here on our bikes by three-thirty at the latest."

"And we could work two hours, at least," I stuck in. I figured my afternoons were usually pretty free, except when I had to baby-sit the twins.

"Two or three afternoons a week," Lauren added.

Alice drummed her fingers on the back of a chair. "It *is* a bit unusual hiring kids so young, but in this case, I think it's okay. And since there would be two of you, that should be enough time. I could only pay you three-fifty an hour each, though. . . ."

"So for two days a week, two hours a day, it would take me . . . um . . . seven weeks — not quite two months! Then the bed would be mine!" Lauren sure breezed through *those* calculations!

Alice nodded approvingly, definitely impressed. "You're interested in the zebra rocker?" she asked me. "It's only a copy of an older one — " That was okay, because the twins weren't going to know the difference. "But it's sturdy and very well made,"

Alice assured me. "It's forty-five dollars."

"A little over three weeks for the rocker," Lauren informed me.

"We're all set then?" Mrs. McWhinny clapped her hands together. "When can you girls start?"

"Tomorrow afternoon, I hope," Lauren said.

"We'll call you if we have a problem with our parents," I told Mrs. McWhinny.

"Why don't you call anyway?" she said. "Just so I'll know for sure. The shop's in the telephone book, and I'll leave my answering machine on."

"It's a deal!" Lauren said happily, and shook Alice's hand. I did, too.

"Should we take a quick look next door at Bernice's?" Kate asked as we edged between piles of furniture toward the door of the store. "Just to be certain that you've found the bed you really want, Lauren?"

"It's the only bed for me," Lauren said firmly.

Suddenly Alice snapped out of her absentmindedness to bark, "Bernice Flanders is . . . is impossible!"

Kate raised an eyebrow at Lauren and me. "Talk about competitive — just because they both happen to own a secondhand furniture store?" she whispered.

But I thought it might be more than that. First of all, Alice didn't seem like the competitive type. And right now she was looking sad, rather than mad. She shook her head slowly a couple of times, as if she were trying to forget something . . . or maybe, in Alice's case, *remember* something!

What could have happened between Alice and Bernice? I mean, their stores couldn't have been any closer unless they were *combined*! And if Bernice felt the way Alice did, it must have made for some pretty uncomfortable situations. Can you imagine what they'd have to do to avoid running into each other every day?

"We don't really have time, anyway — it's getting kind of late," Patti was saying reassuringly for Alice's benefit.

Once we got outside, Lauren looked at her watch. "Yipes! It *is* late! I told Mom I'd defrost some lasagna for dinner! I'm going to ride on ahead, okay?"

"Sure," I said. "I'll call you later."

Lauren nodded and jumped on her bike. Kate, Patti, and I waved as she sped away, hunched over her handlebars. Kate looked at Patti and me. "I think this is an excellent idea, if I do say so myself," she told us. "It'll give Lauren something nice to plan for when she's in her bedroom on Brio Drive."

"You did a nice thing, too, Stephanie," Patti said warmly. "It was terrific of you to volunteer to keep her company at Alice's."

"It'll be fun," I said. "Plus good experience." I'm going to design *the* most awesome clothes when I'm older, and sell them in my own boutique, so the sooner I learn about business, the better.

"Besides," I told Kate and Patti, "what are friends for?" Now all I had to do was convince my parents. . . .

But Mom and Dad were terrific about it.

"I guess a few hours a week wouldn't interfere with your schoolwork, as long as it's not on days we need you to baby-sit," my mom said at dinner that night. "What do you think, Ron?"

"I think it's very generous of you to work toward a present for Emma and Jeremy, honey," my dad said, patting me on the shoulder.

Actually, I was still feeling a little guilty about the way I'd acted toward the twins at first. But after having been an only child for my whole life, suddenly after eleven years I was faced not only with a baby brother, but a baby sister, too. So it's only natural that it took me a while to adjust, right?

Now that they're older and have real personalities, I'm starting to think they're kind of neat. Like Jeremy is always in a good mood, laughing and gurgling to himself. And Emma sounds as though she's practically ready to talk! She has very definite likes and dislikes — she takes after me — and she's quick to let you know about them! But I was sure they were *both* going to like the zebra from Alice's.

"You'll need some working clothes, Stephanie," Dad went on. "What about those checkered pants you showed me last weekend at the mall?"

"The overalls at Just Juniors?!" I shrieked.

"Why don't we drive over there tonight?" Mom suggested. "It'll give the twins a relaxing ride before bedtime, and you'll have a new outfit to wear for your first day at work, Stephanie."

I have to admit — my parents can really be cool!

Chapter
3

Lauren's mom and dad went along with the idea of her working at Alice's, too, as long as she kept her grades up. But we didn't have a chance to talk it over until lunchtime the next day. When I got back from the mall Monday evening it was too late to call Lauren.

And we didn't bike to school together on Tuesday, because it was pouring down rain. Then Mom had trouble with her car, and I got to class just as the last bell was ringing. Needless to say, Mrs. Mead doesn't look kindly on us passing notes in class, so we had to wait until we were in the cafeteria for Lauren to give us a report.

"I explained about the iron bed, and how it's the same age as our house, and how perfect it would look in my room. Not to mention the size problem with the bunks." Lauren waved one of her long legs to show that she meant *her* size, not room size.

"Then Dad started to say how sorry he was, but we couldn't really begin to think about buying new furniture until we'd finished patching up the house. Then *I* told them about the afternoon job at Alice's to pay for the bed, and maybe even some other stuff that we might need. And Mom and Dad were totally surprised that I'd thought it all through so well. They looked at each other, and Dad said, 'Our little girl is growing up, Ann' — corny but nice. And my mom said that Roger would have to take more responsibility for chores around the house while I'm at the shop," Lauren finished with a pleased grin. Roger is Lauren's older brother — he's in high school.

"That's only fair," Kate said. "You had to do *his* chores all those months he was having basketball practice, Lauren."

"What about your parents, Stephanie?" Patti asked me.

"They were kind of excited about it," I said. "In fact, they decided to rush right out and buy me these overalls for my first day on the job." The overalls are that velvety kind of corduroy, covered with teeny gray and white checks, and I was wearing them with a bulky red turtleneck.

"Great outfit, Stephanie!" It was Tracy Osner

27

from 5A — she was standing a couple of kids behind us in the lunchline with Robin Becker, who's in 5B with us. "Hey, didn't I see you guys yesterday at the mini-mall on the Loop? The one with the new Video Connection?"

"That was us — where were you?" Kate asked.

"In the dry cleaner's with my big sister," Tracy replied. "What were you doing there, renting a movie? It doesn't look like you have a tan." We all giggled at the thought of us wearing sun goggles in Tanfastic, catching some rays.

"No, we were looking at a bed in that furniture store, Alice's Attic," Lauren said.

"Does she have anything good? I could use another bookcase for my room," Robin said.

"You bet — lots of good stuff. And we'll be working there a few afternoons a week for a while, helping Mrs. McWhinny. You ought to drop by," I said.

"You're kidding!" said Tracy. "You've got *real* jobs?"

"Mmm-hmm. Stephanie and I," Lauren said. "To pay off the furniture we've picked out."

"What a great idea!" said Tracy. "That way you can choose what *you* want, not what your mom wants, and — "

"Sshhh," Lauren suddenly warned us under her breath. "Ginger again!"

But Ginger made a wide detour around us, grabbed a carton of pineapple-grapefruit juice off the counter, and headed for a far corner of the cafeteria with her tray.

The lunchline moved forward and Lauren whispered, "Do you think she heard us?"

"Who cares?" said Kate.

"I care!" Lauren said. "I don't want her to know *anything* about my life!" As I said before, Ginger had been pretty mean to Lauren. "Plus, she probably thinks having to *work* for something is gross!" Lauren continued. "She and Christy would laugh their heads off about it."

"I'm sure she wouldn't bother to listen to our conversation," Patti said soothingly.

"Yeah, we're really not even worth noticing," I said, watching Ginger unload her tray and rearrange her lunch on the table in front of her. "Still no Christy?" I added. Ginger had stuck the empty tray on the chair next to hers, so she obviously wasn't expecting anyone to sit there.

"You were right yesterday, Stephanie. Christy must be sick," Kate said.

But Patti was shaking her head. "No, there's

Christy in the lunchline. And she doesn't look sick."

Lauren, Kate, and I all turned around to scope out Christy in line. She was staring hard at Ginger and chewing unhappily on her bottom lip.

"She looks upset," Lauren said.

"I wonder what's going on?" I added, noticing that Christy was wearing her hair in a side-ponytail, and Ginger was wearing hers parted in the middle. Not only that, but Christy had on a dark green argyle vest over gray pants, and Ginger was wearing a yellow sweater over a striped miniskirt and tights. So they hadn't even spoken on the phone the night before to coordinate their get-ups!

Back when the six of us worked on the float for the Homecoming parade, Ginger came down with chicken pox at the very last minute, and she was plenty peeved that Christy had gone on the float without her, believe me! But they'd patched things up right away. What could have happened since then?

"Ginger dumped *me*, and now . . . maybe she's dumping Christy!" Lauren said thoughtfully. "That must be it!"

"But why would Ginger dump Christy?" Patti asked sensibly.

"I don't know," I said. "Maybe Christy had her clothing allowance cut?" Kate giggled.

"I wonder who's next on her list of one and only friends?" Lauren said.

"What about Barbara Paulsen?" Kate asked.

Barbara's in 5C with Ginger and Christy. She's cute and easy to get to know, but . . . "Barbara doesn't dress cool enough for Ginger," I said.

Lauren agreed with me. "Kathy Simons is a possibility, don't you think?" Kathy is a blue-eyed blonde in 5A. "She's definitely into clothes — and boys!"

Kate shook her head. "Kathy and Ginger would be fighting it out in five seconds!"

I was so busy trying to think of who Ginger's next victim might be that I almost forgot my other piece of news. We'd already sat down at our regular table in the cafeteria and were digging into our chili dogs — then it came to me. "Remember Alice asking us to call her answering machine at the shop?" I said.

Lauren, Kate, and Patti nodded.

"Well, when Mom and Dad said it was okay for me to work there, I wanted to call Alice and tell her so she wouldn't give our jobs to someone else. Guess what I found in the telephone book when I looked her up? The listing was for 'Alice McWhinny/Bernice Flanders Furniture Bargains'!"

"You mean they used to be partners?" Kate said.

"Right! The two of them must have built a wall

right down the middle of the store!" I said.

"Alice said that Bernice was impossible, but she must have been *possible* at one time," Patti said, wiping some chili off her chin.

"I wonder what happened," said Kate.

"*I* wonder what happened with Ginger and Christy," Lauren said. "Check this out."

Christy was standing stock-still in the center of the cafeteria with her tray. She was gazing mournfully at Ginger sitting in the corner. I guess Christy was hoping Ginger would glance up at her. But Ginger didn't. She picked up her chili dog and took a dainty bite, as though she didn't have another thing on her mind.

Christy's shoulders slumped. She sighed and headed over to the table where Tracy and some other girls were sitting.

"Not that I think Christy's so great," Lauren said. "I mean, she's all right. She was a pretty good sport about working on the float with us — once Ginger was sick. She just doesn't have good sense when it comes to friends. Still — right now I almost feel sorry for her."

"Me, too," said Patti. "Friends should always talk things out if there's a problem."

And Ginger was obviously not talking. She was still eating her lunch as if she didn't have a care in the world. On the other hand, it didn't look as though she had a friend in the world, either. The nearest person to her was Karla Stamos, and she was a whole table away with her head buried in a notebook.

Thank goodness *I* have friends — three of the best! I pulled my little sketchpad out of my tote and flipped it open, then I handed it to Lauren.

"I made another drawing of your room with the new bed in it," I told her.

"Wow! It's going to be perfect!" Lauren exclaimed, looking at my sketch. "And I like just where you put it, too, between the two windows. Plus, my desk looks great in that corner."

Then we started getting excited about our jobs, and talked about ways for Lauren and me to get Alice's Attic organized so that customers could actually see *separate* things when they walked into the store, instead of just a huge jumble of "junque." (That's the way some people in the secondhand furniture business spell "junk" — they think it looks classier.) And we forgot all about Ginger and Christy for the moment.

We had a test in social studies after lunch, so the afternoon flew by. As soon as the final bell rang at three o'clock, we were out of there! Kate had her Video Club, so she rushed down the hall to the art studio. And the Quarks were meeting at the university biology lab to use its fancy equipment.

When Patti, Lauren, and I walked out of the building, one of the small school buses was parked at the curb to taxi the Quarks kids to the lab. Robert Ellwanger and some of the other boys were climbing aboard.

"Good luck!" Patti told us as she veered across the lawn.

"Aren't you going on the bus?" Lauren asked her.

"I promised Walter Williams I'd drive over early with him in his mom's car and help him set up. He's so short that he has trouble adjusting the big microscope," Patti replied.

"Hey, Walter! Mrs. Williams!" Patti waved at a brown car waiting on the corner.

Walter Williams lives in the house behind mine, and he's a genius. He's also a fourth-grader who's young for his grade — he's only eight — and he's about half Patti's height. Frankly, it's not great for her image to hang around with him. (Once Walter was convinced he was in love with Lauren, and it was super embarrassing. But that's another story.) Anyway, if Patti thinks someone needs help, there's no stopping her. . . .

Which must have been pretty much what Lauren

was thinking, because she murmured, "You know, Patti really is nice."

"Sometimes almost too nice," I agreed.

Lauren suddenly looked at her watch. "We have to get to work!"

It had stopped raining by then, so Lauren and I caught a ride with Roger to my house to pick up my bike, which we stuck in the trunk of Roger's car. Then we drove to Brio Drive for Lauren's bike, and the two of us raced up Hillcrest to the Loop and Alice's Attic.

Our first real job! When we got there, Alice wrote our names in a blue notebook and asked us to keep track of the days and hours we worked. Then she explained what she wanted us to do.

"Customers always come first. If there are any in the shop, naturally we're here to take care of them. But when you have some free time, I'd like you to help me neaten up a little. I have a lot of . . . *things*, and we should be able to find spaces for all of them with a little thought. . . ."

It sounds easy enough, right? But if you could have seen this place! Some of that stuff looked as though it hadn't been dusted in five or ten years — maybe, never! In fact, the old dirt seemed kind of *glued* on, so Lauren and I decided to wash what we could. There was a little washroom at the back of the store where Alice kept paper bags and other wrapping supplies.

We carried one or two things at a time through the Attic's maze of furniture to the sink — we had to be careful, because most of the stuff we were hauling around was breakable. I'd wash, Lauren would dry, and then we'd carry it back. I counted forty-two items on a *single* shelf — from little china salt-and-pepper shakers shaped like bunches of grapes, to a pale green glass punch bowl with eight matching cups. Just getting the punch bowl clean took forever!

Once we finished washing, we dusted and wiped the shelves and arranged all the larger things on the bottom ones. We put the smaller things on the top shelves because they looked pretty and they'd be easier to reach that way.

Let's just say that when Alice asked us if we wanted to take a break at four-thirty, we'd been working every second since we'd gotten there, and had barely straightened three of the shelves on *one* wall! Anyway, Alice called a time-out and sent us to a little deli half a block away for Cokes.

On our way back, Lauren and I had just turned into the parking lot carrying our Cherry Cokes, when a gray car pulled up in front of the little wooden barn at the end.

"Hey, I think that's Robin Becker!" Lauren said. "Robin!" she called as the car door swung open.

But the yellow door at Bernice's Basement was opening, too, and a reddish-brown head appeared.

Lauren and I stopped dead in our tracks. "Ginger *again*!" Lauren said in a strangled voice.

"Ginger," I echoed not a second behind her.

"Ro-binnn! I bet we have just what you're looking for *raht heah* in Bernice's Basement!" Ginger yelled in her heaviest southern accent.

We? I thought.

Ginger glanced at us briefly and her mouth turned down at the corners.

"Did she say 'we' or am I just having a bad dream?" Lauren asked.

"If you are, I'm having it, too," I said. I was definitely having a hard time believing my own eyes.

Ginger had a firm grip on Robin's sleeve and she was kind of dragging her along toward Bernice's open door, and Mrs. Becker was following. "Ya'll come right on in!" Ginger said.

And Mrs. Becker had to go along.

Chapter
4

Ginger Kinkaid — working?! It didn't make sense! Her mother bought her everything she could possibly want, and if her mother didn't, then her dad certainly would.

"Yeah, remember that hundred-dollar denim jacket with the rhinestones and fringe from Just Juniors?" Lauren said as she shoved a rusty old ice-cream maker into the corner of a bottom shelf. "When Ginger didn't win the jacket for selling the most tickets to the school raffle, she just waltzed right out and bought one exactly like it!"

"And that fabulous hand-knit sweater at Dandelion that she *knew* I wanted? She got her dad to rush over there after school and beat me to it!" I said. "And it was red, black, and white, too!"

"So what's Ginger doing at Bernice's?" Lauren said.

"There's only one explanation I can think of," I said. "Bernice must be a relative of Ginger's. . . ."

"Alice says Bernice is impossible, and we *know* Ginger is, so that fits," Lauren said, nodding. "You think Ginger is helping her out? Maybe . . ." Ginger isn't known for being helpful.

Just then Robin and her mom showed up at Alice's. And Robin told us what we were having such a hard time believing: "Ginger's working part-time for Bernice, two afternoons a week after school!"

Just like us! But why?

"I thought Ginger spent every second of her spare time shopping for herself!" Lauren whispered to me.

Actually, working in a store is the next best thing to shopping for yourself, don't you think? Plus, you get paid for doing it! I enjoy helping other people shop. Like right now with Robin. I'd been to her house a few times, so I sketched her room from memory and drew in the bookcase she had her eye on at Alice's — it was about five feet tall with rounded trim at the edges and a scalloped top.

"Seeing the way it'll look in my room makes all the difference, doesn't it, Mom?" Robin waved my sketch under her mother's nose. "It's exactly what I need!"

Mrs. Becker agreed with her. "You know, it does look nice!" Mrs. Becker said. "And I like that little oak magazine rack, too. I think we'll take the rack as well as the bookcase, Mrs. McWhinny."

Lauren figured out the tax and total, and Mrs. Becker paid for them. The two of us helped Robin and her mother load the furniture into their car.

The Beckers were pleased, and Alice was pleased, too.

"You're so fast with your math, Lauren. And that sketching is very smart, too, Stephanie. You're both born salespeople."

I smiled a big smile. I was having fun.

But Lauren wasn't! "I think I have to quit," she murmured after we'd signed out in the blue notebook and said good-bye to Alice.

"Quit! Why?" I asked. Working at Alice's was turning out to be a lot of fun. And it was going to pay for a really neat iron bed for Lauren, and a rocking zebra for me (and the twins). *I* didn't want to quit. But I probably would if Lauren did — I'd get lonely with just Alice around. "Don't you like the job?" I asked.

"The job's fine," Lauren said as we headed toward the Attic's door. "But I hate doing the same thing that Ginger is doing. Especially when she's doing it about ten feet away! I know she'll make trouble for me somehow."

As we peeked through the dusty window (we really should wash it, I thought), we saw Ginger walk over to her bike — she'd leaned it against a lamppost. She unlocked it, climbed on, and pedaled across the parking lot toward the Loop exit.

Then Lauren and I left Alice's.

"See?" I said. "There's no reason we ever have to come face to face with Ginger again. She gets here before we do, and we'll let her leave first," I continued. "She'll turn left on the Loop, we'll turn right toward Hillcrest. And that's that!" I said cheerfully. Deerfield Lane, where Ginger lives, is in the opposite direction from Hillcrest.

"She's not turning left," said Lauren.

Sure enough, Ginger was turning right, away from Deerfield.

"She's stopping off at the deli for a Coke?" I guessed. "Anyway, why does it matter?"

"Oh, I don't know," muttered Lauren. "It just bugs me. I don't trust that girl. Come on, let's make sure!" Lauren scrambled onto her bike and I jumped on mine. I didn't know what the big deal was, but I could tell it was important for Lauren to find out, and since I'm her friend . . .

We sped across the parking lot, close on Ginger's tail. Too close!

"Slow down — we're going to roll right over her!" I warned Lauren. "I can practically read the tag on her backpack. Besides, here's the deli and she's going to turn in. . . ."

But Ginger didn't turn in at the deli. She pedaled quickly along until she reached the second stoplight — *our* stoplight, the one at Hillcrest. Then she stuck her arm out to signal a right turn.

Lauren and I had stopped a few car-lengths back, trying to stay out of sight.

"Now she's heading down Hillcrest," Lauren said. "Where's she going?"

"We'll soon find out," I said.

We trailed Ginger past Lauren's turnoff on Brio Drive, and Ginger still kept going, past Lenox Road, Birchwood Circle, and Eagle Lane.

By now, I was definitely getting tired of playing detective. I mean, we'd been in school all day until three, then worked really hard at Alice's for two hours, and we still had homework to do that night. I was worn out. Plus, I was pretty sure I'd figured out where Ginger was going: probably to Main Street, to Charlie's Soda Fountain for one of those chocolate shakes I'd been dying for the day before.

I was just going to say so to Lauren when Ginger

made a sharp left turn. I was so surprised that I almost tipped over! Lauren was, too.

"Ginger's turning onto Mill Road!" she cried, screeching to a stop on the shoulder. Mill Road is Patti's street. "Come on," Lauren said.

We zoomed across Hillcrest and up Mill Road until we were almost even with the Jenkinses' driveway. Then we got off our bikes, pushed them into the hedge, and crawled in ourselves to peer out at Patti's house from between the branches.

"She's here!" Lauren said. "That's Ginger's bike beside the front steps! I can't believe it! Patti is Ginger's next victim!"

"But why?" I whispered. Patti's just not Ginger's type. And Ginger doesn't pick her friends just because they're *nice*.

Lauren shrugged. She was as flabbergasted as I was. "Maybe after hanging around with Christy so much, Ginger decided she'd like to be friends with one of the smartest kids at Riverhurst for a change."

"Or maybe Ginger's here for some other reason entirely," I said hopefully. "Like she's trying to sell raffle tickets or something."

"What raffle?" Lauren said. "We'd know about it."

"Girl Scout cookies?" I was clutching at straws. Lauren sniffed. "Ginger — a Girl Scout!"

43

"I'm sure Patti will tell us all about it tomorrow, and we'll have a good giggle about how crazy we were to imagine her saying more than ten words to Ginger!" I said.

Right about then, a green car rolled up Mill Road, slowed down near the hedge, and turned into the Jenkinses' driveway.

"That's not Patti's mom's car," Lauren whispered. And Patti's dad drives a van. The sun was setting so it was getting kind of shadowy in the driveway. But it wasn't so dark that we couldn't see the driver really clearly.

"Mrs. Kinkaid!" Lauren murmured.

Was the whole Kinkaid family friendly with the Jenkinses all of a sudden? That would really be strange. But it was starting to drizzle and I wanted to get home.

"I'm cold," I said to Lauren. "Let's get out of here."

My hair is thick, dark brown, and sort of wavy. As soon as it's the slightest bit damp, I get world-class frizzies. Which is what happened that evening. But I've found a recipe for a great conditioner made of honey, olive oil, eggs, and other good stuff that calms it right down.

I mixed up some conditioner after dinner —

sometimes my dad teases me and says it smells so interesting that maybe it should *be* dinner. Ha-ha.

While I was grooming *myself*, I decided I might as well groom Cinders, too. Cinders is my cat — brother to Kate's Fredericka, Patti's Adelaide, and Lauren's Rocky. He's coal black with kind of medium-length fur. *He* has problem hair, too. It's not curly like mine, but it's just long enough to get tangled. So I bought a special metal comb for him at Pets of Distinction, and every few days I comb the knots out of his fur.

I was sitting in my room, working on Cinders' head — and trying to keep him from licking the conditioner out of mine — when my private phone rang.

"It just has to be Patti!" I told Cinders. He scooted hastily under my bed as soon as I reached for the phone. He'd had enough of Stephanie's Kitty Salon for one evening.

But it wasn't Patti, after all. It was Lauren.

"She called me," Lauren said.

"I knew she would!" I said. "So what's with the dreaded Ginger Kinkaid?"

"Patti didn't mention Ginger," Lauren said. "She just asked how our first day at work was."

"Hmm. That's weird. This morning Patti was saying how friends should talk about everything. But maybe she wants to tell us about Ginger in person."

45

"Yeah, that's probably it," Lauren said, trying to sound convinced.

The four of us always meet on the corner of Hillcrest and Pine Street — Lauren rides her bike down from Brio Drive, and Patti from Mill Road — at about eight-fifteen on school days. That morning, Kate, Lauren, and I had gotten there first, and were waiting for Patti to show up. Lauren told Kate about our seeing Ginger at Patti's the night before.

"Suppose Patti doesn't mention Ginger at all?" Lauren asked. "What do we do then?"

"Well, the four of us haven't had very many major upsets, right?" Kate said seriously.

"Right." Lauren and I nodded.

"And the ones we *have* had were the result of one thing and one thing only," Kate went on. "Not levelling with each other — trying to keep secrets. Like the surprise birthday party you guys insisted on giving me, remember?"

Lauren and I grinned. "You were convinced that we were mad at you, and that we were thinking up ways to cut you out of the Sleepover Friends — " Lauren began..

" — instead of just planning to give you the best surprise party ever," I finished.

"Exactly. And when Patti didn't want to tell us

46

about getting into the Quarks because she was afraid we'd think she was geeky — " Kate said.

" — and we naturally came to the conclusion that she had a crush on a university student — " Lauren went on.

" — and didn't want us 'kids' hanging around, embarrassing her!" I giggled at how totally off base we'd been.

"We could probably think up five or six other examples," Kate said.

"Um-hmm. *Not* talking always gets us into trouble. And Patti knows that," Lauren said.

Kate nodded. "So either she'll tell us about Ginger straight out, or we'll just ask her straight out. Here she comes!"

Patti was pedaling quickly down Hillcrest toward us.

"Hi!" she said brightly as she skidded to a stop between Lauren and me. "Ready to roll?" Nothing about Ginger!

"Anything you want to tell us about yesterday, Patti?" Lauren asked.

"Yesterday?" Patti sounded surprised. "Oh — you mean the meeting at the university lab? It was awesome! We used their microscopes to look at plankton — those tiny sea animals that whales eat? They were enlarged two hundred times, until it was

like being face to face with actual sea monsters —
red, staring eyes, zillions of legs, big hooks . . ."

Kate, Lauren, and I exchanged glances. Then
Kate got right to the point.

"Not about the Quarks," she said. "About Ginger, Patti."

"Yes, we know — " Lauren began.

"You do?" Patti said. I could have sworn that
she looked *happy* about it. "How — "

"For some reason, she has a job at Bernice's
Basement," Lauren said.

"And on our way home from Alice's yesterday
afternoon, we just happened to, uh, notice her turning into your driveway," I fumbled. *Just happened
to notice?* I mean, riding down Mill Road is not exactly a direct route home for either Lauren or me.
Basically, we'd been *spying*.

Patti's face fell. "Oh," she said. "I thought you
meant you'd — " She stopped herself abruptly.

"So what *was* Ginger doing there?" asked Kate.

Patti peered down at her sneakers and looked
really uncomfortable. "Well," she managed at last,
"Mrs. Kinkaid just got a job at the university, working
in the office of the history department."

"The Kinkaids have sure gotten busy all of a
sudden!" Lauren said under her breath.

"She asked my mom if Ginger could wait at our

house yesterday afternoon until Mrs. Kinkaid could pick her up after work."

"Why didn't Ginger just go home?" Kate asked sensibly. "Deerfield Lane is a lot closer to Bernice's Basement than Mill Road is."

Patti shrugged helplessly. "I think she and her mom were going shopping together or something." Patti looked down at her watch. "Oh! It's almost time for the first bell," she said with relief.

As we whizzed toward school, I asked Patti, "So, what did you and Ginger talk about?"

"Oh, nothing much . . ." Patti said vaguely.

"Well, you survived it, and that's that," I said cheerfully. "Right?"

But Patti just sighed heavily and raced ahead of us without answering. Something was definitely *not* right.

Chapter
5

That morning I couldn't help wondering what was bothering Patti — and what it had to do with Ginger. Why wouldn't Patti just tell us?

Kate passed Lauren a note during math — they sit next to each other in the second row in Mrs. Mead's class. As soon as Lauren read it, she leaned forward and stuck the note in my back pocket. I sit right in front of them, in the first row, and Patti is way off in the last seat in the last row.

I unfolded the note very cautiously while Mrs. Mead was watching Larry Jackson solve a problem at the board. I read Kate's small, neat handwriting:

Patti's problem is, she's too nice. She has a hard time saying no to anybody who needs any kind of help. Even Ginger!

Yeah, I thought. That was it. Maybe Ginger was doing badly in school and Mrs. Kinkaid had asked Patti's mom if Patti could help Ginger out! Patti might be too embarrassed to tell us. . . .

Kate's note added:

So all we have to do is remind Patti that no matter what, all for one, and one for all!

That's the Sleepover Friends' motto.

And I know Patti will tell us what the story is, sooner or later. — K.

But at lunch that day, things got even more wacko. Patti turned out to be having lunch with the Quarks, away from school. They were having a quick picnic on the banks of the Pequontic — that's the river in Riverhurst. Then they were going to collect some samples of river water for their project.

This left Kate, Lauren, and me eating in the cafeteria without her. We had barely plopped down at our table when who should slide onto the empty chair next to Kate? No, *not* Ginger, but almost — Christy!

At least Christy wasn't having any trouble talking to us. After a nervous glance at the table in the far corner — where Ginger was already eating, with her back to the rest of the room — Christy jumped right in.

"Hi," she said. "I know we had some problems with the Homecoming float. But it turned out fine, right? And you guys were the first people in Riverhurst to be friends with Ginger, after all — so I thought you might be able to help me out."

"Friends with Ginger" was maybe stretching it a bit . . . but okay.

"Mmm?" Lauren said politely, and Kate smiled encouragingly for Christy to go on.

"Well, I thought maybe you could tell me what's gone wrong!" Christy said unhappily. "One minute Ginger and I were happier than clams. And the next minute, she acted as though she'd never seen me before!"

Lauren gave a sympathetic nod, and Kate cleared her throat before getting down to business. "Have you tried discussing it with Ginger?" she said.

"Of course I have!" said Christy crossly. "But ever since last weekend she hasn't come to the phone when I call. And if she sees me getting within fifty feet of her, she tears off in the opposite direction. I'm certain I haven't done anything to upset her, but I'm beginning to think the situation's hopeless."

Kate had her "Aha!" face on, the one with one eyebrow up and the other down, like that French detective on Channel 6 who's always coming up with the answers to impossible problems.

"Ever since last weekend . . ." Kate repeated slowly. "What did the two of you do together last weekend?"

"Yeah — did you go to the mall? Maybe *you* bought a sweater or something that *Ginger* really wanted," I said, thinking of the time Ginger had made her dad rush out and buy her the red-black-and-white sweater I'd had my eye on!

"Any kind of argument at all, Christy?" Kate said, frowning at me as she continued. "It wouldn't necessarily have to be about clothes or shopping."

But Christy shook her head. "No, I wasn't even here. As soon as school was over on Friday, I went to visit my aunt and uncle in Hampton for the weekend. Ginger and I were best friends when I left. On Sunday, I called her the very second I got back home. Her brother Matt answered the phone, and he said she couldn't talk to me then — she was busy. *She never called back!* When I got to school on Monday, Ginger practically tripped over her own feet trying to stay away from me. And she hasn't spoken a word to me since!" Christy stopped for a moment before adding, "I thought I saw her bike outside Patti Jenkins's house yesterday afternoon. . . ." Wow — Mill Road had been crawling with spies!

"Sorry, Christy — Ginger doesn't exactly talk to the three of us, either," Kate admitted. "But if we hear anything — "

" — we'll let you know," Lauren promised.

"Thanks a million," Christy said glumly. She picked up her tray and headed for Tracy's table again.

"Pitiful," I said in a low voice. "She must have been following Ginger around, too."

"And I was hoping Christy could give *us* some clues as to what was going on with Ginger," Kate said.

"This is all starting to sound familiar," said Lauren. "When Ginger suddenly stopped talking to me, she was already hanging around with Christy. Now she's stopped talking to Christy, and yesterday she showed up at Patti's house. . . ."

"It doesn't sound good," I said.

That afternoon after school, Patti had a dentist appointment. Then she was going to dinner at the China Wall with her parents and Horace — no way Ginger could get at her that evening. Or at least that's what we thought.

Lauren and I weren't working at Alice's Attic again until the next day, Thursday, so she and Kate and I were sitting on the little deck on the roof of the Hunter house, having a snack of Cokes, jalapeño-cheese dip, and barbecued potato chips. Calories? I'd need a calculator!

"Do you see Willie Judd anywhere?" I asked Lauren, who was standing up at the railing that keeps you from tumbling off the roof.

"Nope. I can see his dog, though," Lauren said, gazing down Brio Drive.

"Where?" I said, squeezing up to the railing beside her.

"The yellow one," Lauren said. "He's as homely as Willie is cute." The dog was tall and skinny, with big ears that stuck straight up. It was asleep on the Judds' front sidewalk, where I'd rather have seen Willie out riding his skateboard — too bad for us.

"I think that's the Kinkaids' house, way over there, isn't it?" Kate pointed at a peaked red roof behind us. "I recognize the two tall chimneys."

"I wish I could be a fly on their wall — to find out what's really going on," I said, staring at the two chimneys.

"If you were a fly on their wall, Ginger would probably swat you," Kate said with a giggle. "Anyway, I'm sure this will turn out to be a lot of fuss over nothing."

It didn't take any longer than the next morning, though, to see that Kate was wrong.

Emma and Jeremy were up yelling most of the night before — they both had bad colds — so I had a hard time waking up the next morning. Plus I'd slept with a pillow over my head to muffle their howls, and now my hair zigged where it should have zagged, which meant wetting it down and blowing it dry while I combed the wrinkles out of it.

I really had to hustle because I didn't want to keep everybody waiting on the corner for me. I bolted down some cereal, grabbed my tote, raced out to the garage for my bike, and pedaled like a maniac up Pine Street. Yep, there was Patti at the end of the block — she was wearing her blue wool cap with the yellow stripe. And Lauren — I could see her straight brown hair above the scarf her aunt Beth sent her from Canada, and Kate in her new blue-and-green down jacket . . . Hey, wait a second! A fourth person?!

I could see reddish-brown hair over a red-black-and-white ski sweater. . . . We were riding to school with *Ginger Kinkaid*! I was so freaked out that both my feet slipped off the pedals! What if I turned off Pine Street into the safety of the Martins' driveway and forgot the whole thing? But if *I* felt weird about Ginger, I could just imagine how Lauren must have felt, with their history. Lauren had plenty more reasons to feel creepy about Ginger than I did.

Somehow, my feet found the pedals again and I wobbled past the Martins', past Lauren's old house, past the Beekmans', and made it to the corner at last.

It was a pretty dismal group that waited there.

"Hey," Lauren said in a totally flat voice.

"Hi, Stephanie," Patti mumbled. "Ginger's riding with us."

As if I hadn't noticed!

"Late," Kate commented, climbing onto her bike.

"My hair," I explained.

Ginger hadn't bothered to say anything up to that point, and she didn't say anything then, either. She just narrowed her eyes and stared at my head as though she thought I ought to put a paper bag over it! This was definitely going to be tougher than I'd dreamed.

Chapter 6

"I feel like I'm trapped in one of those fifties science-fiction movies, where the robots are so old-fashioned they only know one or two words," I murmured to Kate and Lauren as we slowed down near the crossing guard at the corner — Ginger and Patti had ridden on ahead of us. "Hey . . . late . . . hair. . . ."

"It was even worse before you showed up," Kate said. "You know how Ginger usually talks non-stop?"

"Yeah, about her all-time favorite subject — herself," I said.

"Exactly. This morning she didn't say a word. Maybe Ginger really *is* upset about something," Kate said.

"She seems to have plenty to say to Patti — take a look," Lauren pointed out.

Ginger and Patti had already locked their bikes at the rack in front of the school and were standing off to one side, deep in conversation. At least, Ginger was deep in conversation — Patti was listening patiently.

"Don't leave Patti alone with her!" Kate warned, shoving her bike into the rack and scrambling around it toward them.

Ginger switched off practically the second we were within earshot. But I thought I heard her say, ". . . you promised."

Then Ginger gave Lauren, Kate, and me a stony stare, turned on her heel, and marched around the school building to the side door.

"Well, excu-use me!" Lauren said to Ginger's back.

Patti smiled weakly.

"Are you all right?" Kate asked Patti.

"Oh — sure," she replied, looking sad and uneasy at the same time.

"What about Ginger?" Lauren said.

"Yeah. You promised her what?" I added, giving it another try.

"I can't . . . really . . ." Patti shook her head and sighed again.

59

"That's all right," Kate said quickly. "It doesn't matter."

"Thanks, guys," Patti said gratefully. The first bell was ringing, so we headed for the front door of the school.

"For what?" said Kate.

"For being such good friends," Patti said shyly, and ran up the steps.

"Well, I guess we're doing *something* right," Lauren said under her breath as we hustled down the hall behind Patti, toward Mrs. Mead's room.

"But we have to stop making her uncomfortable by asking her Ginger-questions," Kate said sternly, with an eye on me. "Whatever's going on, Patti can't talk about it yet."

"I only thought we'd be able to help *more* if we had information," I defended myself. Besides, let's face it — I was *dying* to know what the deal was with Ginger. I had the strong feeling that whatever it was, it was a lot bigger than Ginger getting help with her homework. *Or* being Patti's new friend — they sure didn't seem to be having any fun together!

At lunch, I was completely blown away by something Ginger said: "This chicken chow mein isn't half as good as the stuff we had last night at the China Wall, is it, Patti?"

But first things first. Mrs. Mead's fifth grade got to the cafeteria first that day, then Mrs. Milton's, and last, Mr. Patterson's — Ginger's class. Lauren, Kate, Patti, and I had gotten our chow mein and little bags of those crispy Chinese noodles — not included in my calorie book — sat down at a small table, and started eating. Four chairs, four girls.

Then who should grab an empty chair from the next table and squeeze in between Kate and Patti? Ginger. Have you ever heard of anything so pushy? Without a "Do you mind if I join you?" Not even an "Excuse me" when she stepped on Kate's toes by accident.

Right off the bat, Ginger mentioned the business about the China Wall the night before. She glanced around the table at Kate, Lauren, and me, to make sure we'd all heard her and gotten the point that she'd had dinner with Patti and her family. Then she clammed up again.

So we'd gotten a little of the old, nasty Ginger. Then we got a mealful of the new, silent Ginger. Patti was talking a little about her Quarks project to fill in those mammoth silences, and the three of us babbled about being up on Lauren's roof the day before. Suddenly more chairs thumped down around us, one on either side of mine, and one between Lauren and

Kate. Henry Larkin, Larry Jackson, and Pete Stone plopped down on them.

They're all in 5B with us. Henry's always kidding around, goofing off in class, and thinking up ways to get you to laugh. He's spent practically as much time in Mrs. Wainwright's office as Mrs. Wainwright has — she's the principal. And Henry and Patti sort of like each other, as different as they are.

Larry's one of Henry's two best friends — the other is Mark Freedman. They hang out together most of the time. And Pete Stone is a guy that Lauren liked for a while. He thinks he's really cute. Actually, I guess he *is* cute: wavy, dark brown hair, light green eyes, tall, a good dresser. At any rate, Ginger usually seems to think he's cute, too. Up until that day, every time I'd ever seen her within a mile of Pete Stone, she pulled out that southern accent and drawled away, grinning like the cat in *Alice in Wonderland*.

That day she was different, though. Once Pete had said "Hi" to Kate, Lauren, Patti, and me, he turned all of his charm in Ginger's direction, leaning in front of Kate to say, "What's happening with you, Ginger Cookie?"

I know, I know — "Ginger Cookie" is too corny to live! But it had always worked with Ginger before.

That day she narrowed her eyes, stared at Pete as though he were the most loathsome slug in the world, and growled, "What's that supposed to mean?"

"N-nothing!" Pete fumbled, turning red.

Ginger bounced up out of her chair and snatched up her tray. "Boys make me sick!" she announced. She dumped her tray in the bin and stormed out of the cafeteria.

"Whoa!" said Larry.

Pete just sat there with his mouth hanging open. "What was that all about?" he finally managed to croak.

"I think you've totally lost it, Pete-O," Henry Larkin said, slapping him on the back. "Hey, Patti — where are you going?"

Patti had stood up, too. "See you later," she blurted at us before rushing out of the cafeteria after Ginger.

"I didn't know you guys hung around with Ginger, anyway," Henry said when he'd snapped out of it.

"We don't," said Lauren.

"Girls are weird," Larry Jackson said, shaking his head and spearing what was left of Lauren's cherry cake.

"We might as well go shoot some baskets," said Pete, scraping his chair back and smoothing his hair down as casually as he could.

As soon as the boys had strolled away, I exclaimed, "*Ginger Kinkaid* said boys make her sick?"

"Maybe that's what all this is about," Kate said. "Ginger's upset about some boy! She was too embarrassed to talk to Christy about it. So for some reason she's turned to Patti. And Patti is so nice that she can't say no."

"It's possible. It could even be that the boy decided he liked *Christy* better than Ginger!" Lauren said excitedly.

"Do we have any idea who Ginger likes now?" asked Kate.

"I saw her last week in Charlie's Soda Fountain, sitting at the counter with Michael Pastore," I reported. And Michael is definitely cute — I used to like him myself.

"Michael could have gotten interested in Kathy Simons again and dropped Ginger!" said Kate. "Anyway, how are we going to find out?"

"Easy — Lauren and I are going to be at Alice's after school, and Ginger will probably be at Bernice's — " I began. "All three of us will be riding our bikes to the Loop. So while we don't want to put Patti on the spot by asking *her* questions about *Ginger*, once Patti's gone home I don't mind asking *Ginger* questions."

"I bet she won't answer them," said Lauren.

64

"Sometimes *not* answering at all is as good an answer as yes or no," said Kate wisely.

When school was out, the four Sleepover Friends gathered at the bike rack. And sure enough, Ginger ended up riding back up Hillcrest with us, or at least with Patti. Ginger rode on Patti's far side, leaving plenty of space between herself and Kate, Lauren, and me.

Kate waved good-bye and turned off on Pine Street. Patti stopped at the corner of Hillcrest and Mill Road. "Well . . . see you tomorrow," she said to the three of us who were left.

"See you *later*." Ginger made a point of correcting her.

Whatever that meant, Patti ducked her head and looked so miserable that Lauren and I started jabbering away to each other about our jobs and pretended we hadn't heard. But we didn't pedal ahead — we had work to do.

"Let her make the first move!" I hissed to Lauren. And as soon as Ginger started to roll, I glided up on one side of her, and Lauren on the other.

At first Ginger ignored us. I guess she was hoping we'd get the hint and drop back. But we didn't. The three of us rode in a perfectly straight row past Eagle Lane, Birchwood Circle, and Lenox Road. If Ginger sped up, Lauren and I sped up. If she slowed down, we slowed down, just like those circus acrobats who perform all their tricks on bicycles. For a split second, I was imagining Kate with one foot on my left shoulder and the other on Ginger's right shoulder, and Patti balanced on Lauren's right shoulder and Ginger's left. . . .

That's when Ginger braked, slinging up gravel. Lauren and I skidded to a stop, too.

"So?" Ginger said rudely. "Just what do you think you're doing?"

"Riding up Hillcrest with you," I said, a lot more politely than I felt.

"I'm perfectly capable of riding up Hillcrest by myself," Ginger said.

"Sure you are," said Lauren. "But isn't it nicer to have company?"

"Besides, I thought we could talk," I said. "It makes the ride go faster."

Ginger had started pedaling again, and so had we. "Talk about what?" she said suspiciously.

I shrugged. "The usual stuff," I said. "Clothes, boys . . . Didn't I see you in Charlie's with Michael Pastore last week?"

"What?" Ginger acted as though her thoughts were a million miles away. "Michael? Um . . . yeah. He was waiting for Kathy Simons to show up." She definitely didn't sound as though she cared a single bit.

Lauren and I rolled our eyes at each other behind Ginger's back — so much for that brilliant idea!

"Why did you decide to get a job at Bernice's?" Lauren asked her, changing subjects as we stopped at the light.

"Why not?" said Ginger, making a left turn as soon as the green arrow flashed on. "Nothing better to do," she muttered under her breath.

There's a lot of traffic on the Loop. You really have to pay attention to what you're doing, and it's hard to talk over the rumble of cars and trucks, anyway. So we had to wait until the three of us had turned into the parking lot of the mini-mall before anyone could say anything else.

"Is that all you wanted to know?" Ginger said coolly as we coasted toward the barn at the end of the row of shops.

"Uh . . . sure. Glad we had this . . . uh . . . opportunity to . . . um . . . chat," Lauren floundered. Round one, round two, and round three to Ginger Kinkaid.

All I could think of to add was, "I like your sweater, Ginger." It was red, black, and white, of course.

So what does Ginger do? She drops her bike on

the ground in front of Bernice's and jerks the sweater off over her head. "You like this sweater?!" she growled between clenched teeth. "Then *take* it, because I *hate* it!"

She flung the sweater at me and stalked into Bernice's Basement!

Chapter
7

Lauren and I practically sprinted into the safety of Alice's Attic. We slammed the door closed behind us and stared breathlessly at each other.

"Whew! What is wrong with that girl?!" Lauren said. "She is acting totally wacko!"

I shook my head, absolutely baffled. "She hates this sweater?" I murmured, holding it up by its sleeves. "Why?"

We didn't have any time to discuss it, though. As soon as we had said hello to Alice, two girls from the university stopped by the shop, looking for a chest of drawers for their dorm room. Lauren and I showed them what Alice had. Then a couple walked in, wanting to trade an old, wooden double bed for a wardrobe. And a young couple who had just gotten married was interested in seeing anything Alice had for the kitchen. By the time Lauren and I had dragged out all the pots and pans we could find, figured out prices and sales tax, and made change, we barely had time to straighten a couple of shelves. And all of a sudden it was a quarter to six!

"Oh, dear — I've kept you too late!" Alice apologized. "Your parents will be very annoyed with me. I'll give you girls a ride home."

"That's okay — we have our bikes, Mrs. McWhinny," I told her.

"We'll load them into the back of my truck," Alice said firmly. "I insist."

Lauren and I were too pooped to argue. Alice switched off the overhead lights and the three of us felt our way toward the door. This time it was Alice who gasped and came to a screeching halt just inside the door. She peeked cautiously through the dusty pane. "You don't mind waiting one second longer?" she whispered over her shoulder.

"Of course not," Lauren and I whispered back. But why were we whispering?

I edged over to squint through the bay window in time to see a tall, thin lady with smooth, white hair crossing the parking lot from the furniture store next door. Something told me it was Bernice Flanders herself, wearing a long-sleeved, flowered print dress, and *heels*. I was sure she'd never had a cobweb draped over her head in her whole life!

"What a difference. No wonder she and Alice don't get along!" I whispered in Lauren's ear — she was peering around me.

"Just because Alice is a little messy?" Lauren said. "So what? *I'm* a little messy, and Kate's super-neat, and she's one of my best friends!"

Which was certainly true. I wondered again what had happened between Alice and Bernice to make them split up the business.

"Ginger's bike is gone," Lauren pointed out. So that was one thing we didn't have to worry about.

Bernice climbed into a small green car, turned on her headlights, and zipped out of the parking lot. Lauren and I lifted our bikes into the back of Alice's little brown truck and were home in a flash ourselves.

Patti and Kate were already parked on the corner of Pine and Hillcrest when I got there early the next morning.

"Patti has something to tell us before Ginger gets here," Kate said hurriedly. "We can let Lauren know later."

Finally — we were finally going to be let in on the secret. "Great!" I said. "Maybe it'll explain why Ginger's acting so strange! She pulled her sweater off and *threw* it at me yester — "

"Stephanie!" Kate groaned.

"Sorry," I said. "Go ahead, Patti."

"I just wanted to let you guys know that Ginger will be at the sleepover at my house tonight," Patti said. She sounded so unhappy about it that she could hardly get the words out. Plus, she seemed to have a little cough. Was she getting sick? "And I'll certainly understand if you decide you'd rather not come," she finished.

"Are you kidding?" Kate said brightly. "We wouldn't miss it for the world, would we, Stephanie?"

"Not for the world," I repeated, stretching my lips into what I hoped looked like an enthusiastic smile. Actually, I would rather have gone to a sleepover with the Creature from the Radioactive Swamp, but, hey — the Creature was probably busy that Friday. "I can give Ginger back her dumb sweater," I added.

Patti coughed again. "Thanks," she said. "You're all being terrific."

"All for one and one for all," said Kate. "Are you doing anything for that cough?" The doctor's daughter was deep into a discussion of the best cough cures when Ginger rode up on her bike, scowled at Kate and me, and said, "Ready?" to Patti.

"We're waiting for Lauren," Patti replied reprovingly — good old Patti. Less than a minute later, Lauren zipped across Hillcrest to join us.

"Ginger crossed the street so she wouldn't have to ride with me," Lauren murmured to me once we'd gotten going. "That girl was *dying* to be my *best* friend only a few short months ago. Isn't she something?"

There was something I hadn't really thought of as far as Patti was concerned. I'd thought a lot about how Ginger takes people up — but not how they feel when she drops them with a thud! Lauren — Christy — she'd end up hurting Patti, too.

But not if *we* could help it!

Ginger didn't join us at lunch, thank goodness — we needed some time to ourselves without her breathing down our necks. She and some of the other fifth-graders who are good at pottery were watching Ms. Gilberto do a firing of clay sculptures, and were having sandwiches from the cafeteria in the art studio.

So the four of us ate at our regular table, just like the old days, and Henry and Larry and Mark Freedman squeezed more chairs in around us, and even Willie Judd stopped by for a second — Willie and Larry are cousins. We had a great time.

Kate did whisper worriedly to me at one point,

"I don't think Patti feels very well, do you? She's coughing and she has dark circles under her eyes."

"Too much Ginger," I said gloomily. "It's wearing Patti down. Now the creep is even crashing our sleepover!"

As it turned out, "smashing" might have been a better word than "crashing." Kate and I got to Patti's house — my dad drove us over — just as Roger was dropping Lauren off. So the three of us huddled for a quick conference at the end of the Jenkinses' sidewalk.

"Any words of wisdom about tonight?" Lauren said.

Kate's never at a loss for words. "Yes — we make it as easy for Patti as we possibly can."

"And just how do we do that?" I asked. "Nothing's easy with Ginger around."

"We're as nice as pie to Ginger, of course," Kate said. "Agreed?"

"Agreed," Lauren and I grumbled.

But Ginger made it very, very difficult. Like about the snacks, for example. One of the most important parts of a sleepover is the snacks, right? And the goopier and gloppier, the better.

Ginger watched in disapproving silence as Lauren and I mixed up some of Lauren's special dip: onion-soup-olives-bacon-bits-and-sour-cream. When we'd finished, Ginger rolled her eyes to the heavens and said, "Ick! Have you ever thought about what all that fat does to your skin?"

"Fat?" Lauren said.

"Sour cream, bacon bits — all that stuff is bad for your skin." Ginger lowered her eyes to meet mine. "Not to mention your *hips*."

Nice, hmm?

Kate had brought over a plastic container of her dynamite super-fudge, still warm from the pan. And what did Ginger say as Kate passed it around? "Sugar is poison for your body!"

She turned down blue-corn chips ("too greasy"), Chee-tos (ditto), butterscotch popcorn ("butterscotch is solid sugar"), peanut-butter-chocolate-chip cookies (from my mom — I guess Ginger knew better than to comment), and Dr Pepper floats ("wreck your teeth"). Instead, she asked for club soda and carrot sticks, which was fine, since Patti happened to have those items. But did Ginger have to ruin *our* snacks with her snide remarks?

Anyway, we got the "poisonous" food organized on trays and carried them up to the attic. Patti's attic is a great place to have a sleepover, because you can make all the noise you want without bothering anybody. It's a big open space running across the whole top of the Jenkinses' house, with a pointed ceiling, little round windows like portholes in each of the walls, and crisscrossing rafters. Patti strung the rafters with those tiny, clear, Christmas-tree lights, so when you turn the overhead bulb off and switch the Christmas lights on, it's like looking at the stars.

Patti had already lugged the sleeping bags up there, her radio/tape player, and the Jenkinses' little portable TV, so we were all set. We used the sleeping bags for cushions, and spread the snacks out on an old hooked rug on the floor. I was a little worried about Patti. She seemed really tired. Of course, I didn't blame her!

Lauren reached over, switched on the radio, and tuned it to WBRM. On Friday nights the Riverhurst radio station takes phone-in requests — you know, like "From F. B. to R. L.: 'You're the Only Girl for Me.' " It's mostly high-school kids, but still, it's fun to try to guess who's who. Plus the music is always great, and sometimes we practice the latest dance routines that we've seen on *Video Trax*.

Anyway, that night we heard a couple of songs with no dedications — one was "Shake," from the first Heat album, and "Texas Girls," by the B29s. And that was fine, because at least we didn't have to try to make small talk with Ginger while we were listening.

Then something really weird happened. Rockin' Ralphie, the WBRM deejay, announced, "I just got a request from T. K. to B. B." — that's Tug Keeler and Barbara Baxter. Tug's on the Riverhurst High football team and Barbara's a cheerleader. They've been steadies for years. "This is a song to snuggle up to, folks," Rockin' Ralphie went on. "By the Tru-Tones: 'Always, Forever.' "

"Turn that off!" Ginger thundered so loudly that I spilled dip all down the front of my favorite black-and-white-striped sweat shirt!

"Excuse me?" said Kate, dumbstruck.

"*Off!*" Ginger absolutely flung herself at the radio and punched the "off" button. "I hate that awful, soppy stuff! 'Always, forever your love' . . . *yuck!*"

Wow — I would have thought it was just the kind of sweetsy, romantic song Ginger would have liked. But what happened next was even more amazing.

Patti suggested nervously, "Why don't we watch some TV?"

Kate nodded. "I think that funny old thirties movie called *One Hundred Years of Wedded Bliss* is on Channel 6," she said. Kate practically memorizes the movie schedule as soon as the weekly TV guide section comes out in the Sunday *Riverhurst Clarion*.

But Ginger screeched at Patti, "You *told* them, didn't you? You *told* them, and you gave me your solemn word that you wouldn't! Fink!" Ginger burst into loud sobs, scrambled to her feet, and went charging down the attic stairs. As the four of us just sat there on the sleeping bags, stunned, we heard her wail, "Mrs. Jenkins, I don't want to stay here tonight! Please!"

Chapter
8

Kate, Lauren, and I were the ones who ended up leaving the Jenkinses' that night, not Ginger. But not before we learned a couple of interesting things. One was, whatever it was that Patti wasn't supposed to tell, she had promised her mom, not Ginger.

After Ginger had burst into tears and dashed down the stairs, Patti sighed and followed her. And Lauren, Kate, and I heard Patti saying, "Mom, you asked me not to say anything, and I didn't, not even to my best friends. And I won't, until Ginger is ready to tell people herself."

The other interesting thing was, Mr. and Mrs. Jenkins were getting as tired of Ginger as we were. Right after the door to the spare bedroom banged shut below us, and just before Mrs. Jenkins climbed the attic stairs, we overheard her say, "Philip" —

that's Patti's dad — "I know the child is going through a terrible time, but she certainly isn't helping anything by acting like this."

The three of us were crouching at the top of the stairs, practically holding our breath so we wouldn't miss a word. We dashed back to the sleeping bags on tiptoe and waited for Mrs. Jenkins's head to appear over the banister.

"Girls, I hate to ask you to do this . . ." Mrs. Jenkins began.

"Would it be easier if we took a rain check on this sleepover, Mrs. Jenkins?" I offered.

"Would you mind terribly?" she said, relieved. "Ginger is a . . . little upset . . ." — we'd all agree with that! — ". . . and I think it would be best if she had some time to herself to calm down."

"Like two or three years," Lauren muttered under her breath.

"That's fine," I said. "I'll call my parents and tell them that we'll be spending the rest of tonight's sleepover in the apartment."

The "apartment" is what I call this terrific little cottage Dad built for me in the backyard as a surprise for my last birthday. "You'll need a place to go to get away from the twins from time to time," he said. It's really neat: two pullout couches, a tiny little bathroom, even a midget fridge for sleepover snacks. And a TV for *Video Trax*, of course.

"I guess Patti has to stay here?" Lauren said.

"Yes, I think she'd better," Mrs. Jenkins said. She sounded as sorry about her daughter being stuck with Ginger as we were. "Mr. Jenkins will drive you home. We'll do something fun the next time you're here, to make up for tonight — okay?"

"Great!" the three of us said.

We felt truly guilty about saying goodbye to Patti, leaving her alone with the Horrific Houseguest. Otherwise, we were plenty glad to get out of there! Back at the apartment, safe in my calm, quiet, back-yard, we listed any clues we might have to Ginger's deep, dark secret.

"Ginger says boys make her sick," Lauren began. "That's a *big* switch."

"And she doesn't care about Michael Pastore one way or the other," I went on.

"She's working at Bernice's because she has 'nothing better to do,' " said Kate. "I guess she means because her mother has a job now."

"She hates a perfectly nice red-black-and-white sweater that her father rushed out and bought her because she wanted it so badly," I said, puzzled —

I'd left the sweater folded neatly on the kitchen counter at the Jenkinses'.

"She has a secret that she's afraid Patti will tell us. . . ." said Lauren.

". . . that Mrs. Jenkins knows about, too, probably from Mrs. Kinkaid," Kate said.

"She doesn't like tasty food," Lauren said, standing up to rummage around in my little fridge.

"That has nothing to do with anything, Lauren," Kate scolded.

"Okay, okay — a song about love, and a movie about weddings, both made her crazy," Lauren said, walking back to the couches with a container of fudge ripple ice cream and three spoons.

"So what does it all add up to, Professeur Pierre?" I asked. He's the French detective on Channel 6 whose "aha" face Kate borrows sometimes.

But Kate shook her head. "I don't know." She took a spoonful of ice cream. "Is one of her brothers getting married?"

I guess that *would* cover boys, love, weddings, and secrets, but . . .

"Get real!" said Lauren, throwing a pillow at Kate's head with a giggle. "They're Roger's age!"

"Then I'm stumped." Kate shrugged. "We'll just have to wait for Patti to tell us."

* * *

The next morning I went to the city with my parents and the twins. First we checked out the natural history museum and the planetarium. Then Mom and I went shopping — she bought me a pair of fabulous red-and-black Western boots — while Dad took the twins to the children's zoo in their double stroller. We spent the night at Nana's apartment — Nana and Dan were staying at his house in Maine all that month.

We ate breakfast the next day at Scrumptious, one of my favorite restaurants. They have fabulous waffles with maple ice cream. We strolled all over town, had hot dogs with sauerkraut in the park, and headed back to Riverhurst late that afternoon.

Kate must have been staring out of her living-room window when we drove down Pine Street, because my phone rang just a couple of seconds after I got home.

"What's up?" I said.

"Patti came down with a fever," Kate said. "Mrs. Jenkins called, and my dad went over there last night to see about her. Patti was coughing, too, but Dad says it's just a cold. She's going to stay home tomorrow."

"I hope she's okay," I said.

"She'll be fine. But she could be out of school until Wednesday," Kate reported. "Dad thinks she probably caught it because she was a little run-down."

"She's worn out from dealing with *Ginger Kinkaid*!" I said.

"Exactly!" said Kate. "That's why we have to get to the bottom of this, once and for all."

"You bet we do!" I said. "But how? Sit with Ginger at lunch tomorrow and tell her if she won't reveal her secret, we'll make her eat fatty junk food?"

Needless to say, Ginger had lunch alone on Monday because Patti was home with her cold. And surprisingly, it was Bullwinkle who pointed us in the right direction to solve the mystery. Kate and I rode over to Lauren's house after school that day. She and Lauren and I were hanging out at the Hunters' kitchen table, drinking Dr Peppers and trying to come up with ideas to solve the Ginger problem.

Suddenly, not far away, a couple of dogs started barking really loudly.

"Is that Bullwinkle making all that noise, Lauren?" Kate said crossly, setting down her Dr Pepper.

"No, he's asleep near the back steps," Lauren said. She peered through the window at her backyard. Then she changed her tune. "He *was* asleep! Now he's not there!" Lauren ran into the living room to stare out the window toward Willie Judd's house. "Oh, no! Bullwinkle breakout!"

By now, I know what the drill is when Bullwinkle escapes almost as well as Lauren and Roger do. You race after him, through puddles and hedges and gardens, and you pile onto him because he's so enormous — that's the only way to slow him down. And I was wearing my favorite sweater that day — a red-and-white one with little yellow squiggles. Oh, well. Sleepover Friends to the rescue!

We snagged our jackets off the back porch on our way through — I mean, it was warm enough for just sweaters right now, but who knew how long the capture would take? — and practically fell down the back steps. Bullwinkle may be big and kind of clumsy, but he can move pretty fast when he wants to.

But Bullwinkle wasn't at the Judds' when we got there. The only one at home was Willie's dog. He was stretched out on the Judds' front steps, snoozing.

"The Randazzos?" Kate suggested.

But the Randazzos weren't home, either. We could hear their dachshund barking its head off inside. We peeked over their back fence in case Bullwinkle had managed to squeeze under it somehow, but he was nowhere to be seen.

So we went back to the street and stared up and down Brio Drive, trying to decide where to go next. Then a little kid on skates came rolling up the sidewalk toward us.

"Don't you own that big black dog?" he asked Lauren.

"Yes! Have you seen him?" Lauren asked anxiously.

"You bet. He was turning down Hillcrest just a few minutes ago," the little boy said.

"Oh, no!" Lauren shrieked. "He could get run over!" She ran back to her house, jumped on her bike, and shot away from us so fast it was like she was jet-propelled!

Kate and I didn't catch up with her until she finally slowed down for us near Eagle Lane.

"Two cars had to stop for him, but he made it across Hillcrest safely," Lauren said breathlessly. "I just saw him turn in on Pine Street."

"Pine Street?" Kate asked.

Lauren nodded. "I think he's probably going back to our old house."

Poor Bullwinkle! I guess he missed the place on Pine Street as much as Lauren did. But he wasn't going to find his family there — he was just going to find an empty house.

Or was he?

"Lauren, there's a moving van outside your old house!" Kate said the second we turned onto Pine Street ourselves.

Lauren shook her head. "It must be at the Kennans', next door. They haven't been living there long — maybe they found another house they like better."

"Lauren, it *is* at your house!" I told her.

Lauren's pedaling was getting slower and slower until it stopped altogether.

"It *is* — it is at my house," she said to herself so softly that I barely heard it. "But Dad didn't say anything to me about anyone moving in here!" Lauren started pedaling again, faster and faster.

"Maybe it happened overnight," Kate said, struggling to keep up.

But it takes a while to pack up all your stuff, as Lauren knew, since she had just done it when her family moved.

"Maybe your dad was so relieved to finally find somebody to sell the house to that he . . . he didn't want to jinx the deal by talking about it until it was really final!" I said, huffing and puffing.

"I want to know exactly what's going on here!" Lauren said, her face like thunder. "I want to know who these people are!"

She braked her bike suddenly, so close to the

side of the van that I thought she was going to ram into it!

In the back of the van, a young guy was passing furniture and cardboard boxes down to a man on the ground. One of the boxes said "Everyday Dishes." Another said, "Glasses."

"Who's moving in here?" Lauren asked a big man in brown overalls who was carrying a clipboard. "Whose stuff is this?"

"This belongs to the — " he checked his clipboard. "To the Kinkaids. Friends of yours?" he added cheerfully.

Chapter
9

The *Kinkaids*! Lauren couldn't have looked more stunned than if the guy had said the Creature from the Radioactive Swamp was moving into her house with his whole family! And who could blame her? Lauren's least favorite person, eating in her old kitchen, watching TV in her old den, *sleeping in her old bedroom!*

I know Kate was shocked, too. Ginger, as practically a next-door neighbor — what could be worse? At least my house is at the other end of Pine Street, about as far away from Ginger as I could get without living on another street altogether! Which brought me to the real question: Why were the Kinkaids moving out of their house on Deerfield Lane, which is a lot bigger than this one? I mean, Ginger has two older brothers!

"Do you think *she's* here?" Lauren said, her voice full of dread.

"Uh-uh. I bet she's working at Bernice's this afternoon," I said confidently. But I really had no idea.

"Lauren, what about Bullwinkle?" Kate was saying. "Lauren!" she repeated sternly. "We have to find your dog!"

Lauren came out of her daze long enough to say, "We'd better check the garage. He liked taking naps in there."

We propped our bikes against the oak tree next to the sidewalk, just the way we'd done it hundreds of times while Lauren still lived there. Then we trudged up the driveway toward the garage in back. It felt pretty sad that this wasn't Lauren's house anymore.

We walked past the closed wooden sliding doors, around the side of the garage to the back. There's a loose board back there that Bullwinkle used to push aside with his nose, so he could squeeze inside.

"What if he's not in there?" Lauren said to Kate. "You look — I can't."

"I didn't bring my glasses," Kate said.

So I put *my* eye to the crack and squinted into

Lauren's old garage. The sun was shining through a window onto a couple of chairs, some piles of boxes, and — Bullwinkle. He was dozing in a corner with his round black head resting on a rolled-up rug.

"He's in there," I reported.

"Whew!" We all breathed a sigh of relief.

Lauren scrunched down to push the board aside and climb into the garage to drag Bullwinkle out. Kate and I went to borrow a piece of rope from the moving men. Once Bullwinkle was captured, Lauren tied one end of the rope to his collar and the other end to her bicycle frame. The three of us started slowly up Pine Street with Bullwinkle trotting along behind.

"It's the Kinkaids, all right," Lauren said glumly. "There were some boxes in the garage marked 'Ginger's Bedroom.' "

"So this is it?" I said. "This is Ginger's deep, dark, secret? Big deal! Lots of people move!"

"It *is* a big deal," said Lauren crossly. "It's *my* house she's moving into!"

"But why wouldn't she want anyone to know?" I persisted. "It doesn't make sense."

"Maybe the address isn't fancy enough for her," Kate said snippily, since she lives on Pine Street, too.

"I guess Dad didn't tell me because he knew

how I'd feel about it," Lauren was muttering. We'd turned onto Hillcrest by then, and a car horn gave a couple of blasts right behind us.

Kate glanced over her shoulder. "Now's your chance to ask him, Lauren," she said, "because here's your dad."

Sure enough, Mr. Hunter was right behind us. We coasted to a stop as he pulled his car onto the shoulder of the road and jumped out.

"Where did you find Bullwinkle? I've been driving all over the place looking for him. I'm glad you found him before he got hurt."

Lauren looked her father square in the eye. "We found him at Eleven Pine Street, Dad," she said accusingly. "Why didn't you tell me the Kinkaids were moving into our house?" Her bottom lip was sort of quivery. "You could have warned me, at least."

"Oh, honey, I'm sorry," said Mr. Hunter, giving her a hug. "I didn't know myself until yesterday. At first Mr. Blaney just said he might be interested in renting it for some friends."

Renting it — at least the Kinkaids weren't *buying* Lauren's old house. Not yet, anyway.

"Then . . . you girls are going to hear about this soon enough, I'm sure, but I want you to promise me you will not repeat it," Mr. Hunter said sternly.

"We promise," the three of us chorused.

"Mr. and Mrs. Kinkaid are getting a divorce," Mr. Hunter said gravely. "Mrs. Kinkaid and Ginger will move into our old house, and Mr. Kinkaid and the boys will be staying at the house on Deerfield Lane."

Lauren, Kate, and I gasped so loudly that Bullwinkle wagged his tail anxiously.

" 'Sick of boys . . . love . . . wedded bliss' — now it all makes sense," Kate murmured.

"Poor Ginger," I said slowly. I mean, who could wish something as awful as a divorce on any kid?

"How horrible!" said Lauren. "It's bad enough having your parents split up. Do the kids have to be split up, too?"

Mr. Hunter was propping open the trunk of his car to wedge Lauren's bike inside it. "Come on," he said to his daughter. "I'm going to give your escorts a break, and drive you and Bullwinkle home in style."

The big black dog crammed himself into the back seat. Lauren climbed into the front seat with her dad and waved good-bye as they drove away.

Kate shook her head and sighed. "Ginger *definitely* needs a friend," she said.

"But not Patti!" I squawked. "Ginger has practically *killed* her already!"

"Not Patti," Kate said. "Christy — Christy's used to Ginger."

"But Ginger must be too embarrassed to talk to Christy," I pointed out. "The only reason she talks to Patti must be that Patti already knew about the divorce, since Mrs. Kinkaid probably told Mrs. Jenkins at work. And we can't tell Christy — we gave Mr. Hunter our word."

"We'll have to think of another way to get Christy into the picture," said Kate, determined.

On Tuesday, Mr. Patterson's class went on a field trip to Chesterfield, this mansion a few miles up the Pequontic. But Kate and I caught up with Christy before school on Wednesday. She was hanging around near the side door, hoping to bump into Ginger.

As usual, Kate got straight to the point. "We've decided to help you out, Christy," Kate said. "We'll get you and Ginger together, and make Ginger at least listen to what you have to say."

"How will you do that?" Christy asked eagerly. "It won't work in the cafeteria. As soon as Ginger sees me coming, she escapes out the side door. And it won't work before or after school, either. Ginger runs away as soon as she spots me."

"Maybe one of us could go up to her first, get

94

her talking, and then, Christy, you could . . . nope, nope — scratch that." I shook my head. Obviously the only one of us Ginger seemed to be willing to talk to right now was Patti. And she was still out sick.

Then Kate sighed. "There's the sleepover at my house on Friday, I guess . . ."

Wha-a-at?! Not our sleepover again!

". . . and if you'll come, we'll see to it that Ginger is there, too!" Kate said triumphantly to Christy.

YUCK-o! Maybe Christy wouldn't go for it . . . but she *did*!

"Thanks a million," Christy said, smiling for the first time in days. "I'll be there on Friday, for sure!"

Yeah, I thought, thanks a million, Kate. . . . I couldn't come up with anything better, but I still wasn't at all convinced that this plan of hers would work. And, anyway, I was tired of sacrificing our sleepovers to these two's problems! Who were we, the Ann Landers of the fifth grade?

I kept grumbling to myself like this all the way to Mrs. Mead's class, but I still couldn't come up with another plan. I guess Operation Sleepover was really on.

Alice had called Lauren and asked that we only come one day that week, Wednesday, because she was going on a buying trip and was going to close the shop on Tuesday. So Lauren and I were working at Alice's that afternoon after school. Kate was on her way home, so she rode with Lauren and me up Hillcrest, explaining her latest brilliant idea to Lauren.

"So you're telling me that we have to beg a girl we can't stand — " said Lauren.

"Who can't stand us, either," I interrupted.

" — who can't stand us, either, to spend this Friday night at our sleepover! Yuck! Kate, this has got to be one of your worst ideas ever! I know we're desperate, but . . ." Lauren broke off.

"Well, do either of you have any other ideas?" Kate said huffily. "I don't see you guys making lists of possible alternatives!"

Uh-oh. I knew what happened when Kate got like this — there was no backing out! When Lauren and I were silent, Kate went on.

"We'll just tell Ginger that *Patti* wants her to come to the sleepover," Kate said. "That should do it, don't you think?"

Lauren and I nodded.

"Maybe," I said. "But if she still won't?"

"What if Patti's still sick and *she* can't come?" Lauren asked.

Kate pedaled firmly ahead. "She won't be. And

Ginger will *have* to come. We'll just *make* her!" she said grimly. Lauren and I looked at each other and tried not to smile. We were sure glad *we* weren't on the receiving end of Kate's glare!

Right before Kate turned off on Pine Street, she called over her shoulder, "We're getting Ginger and Christy back together again, and that's final!"

Ginger's bike was already locked to the lamp-post outside Bernice's Basement when Lauren and I got there. Instead of walking straight through the green door, I paused long enough to take a good look into Bernice's window.

Bernice's store and Alice's are like night and day, just like their personalities. Where Alice's is wall-to-wall clutter, Bernice has a place for everything and everything's in its place. Her pictures and prints are hung neatly on the walls, not stacked on the floor. Her furniture, even if it *is* missing a leg or two, is arranged the way it would be in a real house. Not like Alice's, with footstools piled on end tables piled on sofas!

"Duck! There's Ginger!" Lauren said suddenly.

Ginger had just stepped through a door in the back of the store, so we faded away from the window and dashed into Alice's.

"Helloooo — may I help you?" Alice was unpacking boxes of new items she had bought in a corner, but when she glanced up and saw us, she said cheerfully, "No, you've come to help *me*, praise be!"

Lauren and I got right to work on the shelves we'd been neatening. While Alice went on with her sorting and unpacking, she asked all about Lauren's bedroom, like what color it was painted, and how large it was, and what furniture Lauren had put in it so far.

Five-thirty rolled around almost before we knew it! Lauren and I had actually cleaned up and rearranged six more shelves. We stepped back to admire them, and talked about what we were going to do the following Tuesday afternoon.

"I can't wait to get my hands on those piles of furniture," I said to Lauren in a low voice. "I think we should group all the chests of drawers together in one part of the room, all the armchairs in another, and maybe actually set up a dining table in the middle, with some of Alice's glasses and dishes off the shelves. So that it looks like it's in a house, not a garage — the way Bernice does it."

Lauren suddenly interrupted. "Just a sec — there are some bits of paper sticking out from behind that vase up there. That one shaped like a cowboy boot, on the second shelf from the top."

I groaned. "I bet it's more packing material." I was too short to see the paper, but I knew only too well that Alice could have stuck *anything* up there. Lauren got a chair and stood on it, trying to reach the vase.

"That's funny," she said, standing on her tiptoes and reaching her arm up as high as she could. "It almost looks like it might be — " She pulled a wad of greenish paper out and jumped off the chair so we could both see it.

"It is!" she exclaimed. "It's money!"

"You're right!" I gasped. "Lots of it!"

"Twenty, forty, sixty . . . one-fifty . . . two-twenty . . ." When Lauren finally stopped counting, she had four hundred and ninety-five dollars!

"Uh, Mrs. McWhinny?" Lauren called out.

Alice popped out from behind a narrow chest of drawers.

"Oh, is it time for you girls to go already? I don't want you to be late for dinner," she said brightly.

"Okay, but first — Lauren found some loose bills on one of the shelves," I said.

"Loose bills? Oh, dear. I'm so absentminded that sometimes I forget to put money in the cash box," Alice said, threading her way toward us through mounds of furniture.

"It's four hundred and ninety-five dollars, Mrs. McWhinny," Lauren said.

"Four hundred and ninety-five dollars!" Alice skidded to a halt. "Why, I haven't made that kind of sale for months! Not since . . . not since . . ." Suddenly her face crumpled. "Oh, dear me."

"Is, uh, something the matter, Mrs. McWhinny?" Lauren asked.

Alice shook her head back and forth, looking really distressed. "Bernice was right all along," she said almost to herself. "Oh, dear me. How could I ever make it up to her? The *things* I said . . . the things *she* said. . . ."

"All friends have misunderstandings sometimes, Mrs. McWhinny," I said soothingly, although I wasn't sure what she was talking about.

"But the best thing about friends," Lauren added seriously, "is that they're always willing to give you a chance to explain."

"You think I should try to . . . talk to Bernice?" Alice said, dabbing at her eyes with a dusty tissue.

"Absolutely!" Lauren and I said at the same time.

"I don't know . . ." Alice collapsed forlornly onto the corner of a faded maroon sofa. Lauren and I stood there uncertainly.

"Uh, can I get you anything?" Lauren asked.

Alice looked up with a faint smile. "No, dear, thank you. I think you've done plenty already. The rest is up to me, I'm afraid." There was a sudden determined sparkle in her eye.

"Now you girls run along and don't worry about me. There's only one thing to do!"

So Lauren and I got our jackets, signed out in the blue notebook, and said good-bye.

"That money you found seems to have unraveled the mystery of why it isn't 'Alice McWhinny/Bernice Flanders Furniture Bargains' anymore," I said to Lauren as we headed for our bikes. "Do you think they'll make up now?"

"There's a good chance of it," Lauren said, motioning back toward the store. Alice McWhinny was standing on the sidewalk outside Bernice's Basement. As we watched, she took a deep breath, smoothed down her hair, and marched through the yellow door!

Lauren and I gave each other a high-five!

Chapter
10

Mom had some good news for me when I got home — Patti had called! I phoned her back the minute dinner was over.

She was still a little hoarse, but otherwise she sounded fine. "I'm so glad Lauren's dad told you guys about Ginger," she said. "I wanted to talk to you about it so badly, but I'd promised my mom. . . ."

"No problem," I said. "Now we just have to keep our fingers crossed that Ginger will go to Kate's . . ."

"Oh — Kate called me a while ago and explained what was going on. Then, guess who called me — Ginger. She sounded pretty down, and when I asked her to go to Kate's sleepover, she said yes! I have a strong feeling she'll be there on Friday." Patti sighed. "She's really going through a rough time."

When Patti showed up at school the next day, there were promising signs for the sleepover. Ginger actually smiled and said hi to Patti in the lunchline, before marching off to eat by herself.

But I guess she mulled things over that afternoon and decided she couldn't deal with Kate, Lauren, and me, too. Because when all of the Sleepover Friends met on the corner on Thursday — it was Patti's first day back on her bike — Kate reported, "Ginger's *not* coming to the sleepover. Her mother called my mom last night and said they were moving most of their furniture over on Friday, and she was afraid Ginger was going to be too tired to go to a party. And could she come another time?"

"But what about Christy?" Patti asked. "We told her we'd help her."

I nodded. "I feel sorry for Ginger, too. I know she can be really awful sometimes, but she sure needs a friend right now."

"And I think that friend should be Christy, instead of some poor helpless victim who doesn't know any better," Kate said. "Plus, Ginger's almost *my* next-door neighbor. I don't want her looking in *my* direction!"

We all smiled. "You've got a point," Lauren said.

We were coasting down Hillcrest toward school by then.

"So what good will it do to have Christy come to our sleepover on Friday if Ginger stays home? And why would Christy want to, anyway?" Lauren asked.

"We'll just have to figure something out," Kate said. "And we only have one day!"

The next morning, we met on the corner of Hillcrest and Pine as usual. Kate surveyed the three of us with narrowed eyes.

"Well? Does anyone have a plan?" Lauren and I stood there looking down at our sneakers. It wasn't that I hadn't *thought* about it — I had. But I just couldn't come up with anything that seemed to make sense.

Then Patti cleared her throat.

"Um, you guys, if we make sure Christy still thinks Ginger is coming tonight, Christy will show up. Then, what about a nice, friendly game of Truth or Dare?" she said. "It seems to me that we could use a dare to send Christy almost anywhere in the neighborhood. . . ."

Kate grinned. "Like two doors down?" she said.

The four of us looked at each other, smiles breaking across our faces. "Brilliant," I said.

* * *

But our brilliant plan looked a little iffy when Ginger acted cold as ice in the lunchline that day — and Christy saw it.

"Hi, Ginger," Kate said brightly for Christy's benefit, as Ginger pounced on the last carton of cranberry-apple drink. Ginger was wearing her hair in a regular braid, and she glared and sort of flipped the braid away from us, as if we were dirt. Then she hustled over to her corner again.

"Are you *sure* she's coming to the sleepover tonight?" Christy poked her head around Robin Becker to whisper. "Ginger doesn't seem to be speaking to *you*, either."

"No problem," Kate replied breezily. "I *know* we'll get you two together tonight." Well, she wasn't *exactly* lying.

We firmed everything up with Christy when school was over that afternoon.

"My house, at seven-thirty, okay, Christy?" Kate said. "Seven Pine Street."

"All right," Christy said. "And Ginger will definitely come?"

"You'll have your chance to talk to her, we guarantee it," I said.

"Thanks loads. This is great of you guys!" Christy said. "See you later."

"I hope we can pull this off," Lauren said doubtfully as Christy climbed into her mother's car.

"With four great minds like ours?" Kate said. "Piece of cake."

So Christy was coming to Kate's at seven-thirty. Which is why Lauren, Patti, and I were upstairs in Kate's bedroom at seven o'clock, running through the plans for the evening.

"Well, we'll have to have snacks, of course," Lauren said. Trust Lauren to make sure of the snacks!

"Yes, but that won't take very long," Patti said. "We have to kill more time than that to make sure Ginger's settled in at the new house."

"I know," I said. "We could ask Christy to show us how to fix our hair in some new way. That should take a while."

Kate nodded seriously. As usual, she was making a list of our plans. "That should do it," she said. "Then we'll move straight on to Truth or Dare. How are we going to work it? Patti?"

Patti cleared her throat. Thank goodness she was over her cold! I had been worried that her parents might make her skip this week's sleepover because she'd been sick. She had finally convinced them, but she was under instructions not to "overdo it."

"Well, I thought that we should all pick each other first," Patti began. "And we'll each choose

Truth. And the truths we tell will be so totally embarrassing. . . ."

". . . so completely mortifying," Lauren said.

". . . so awful that Christy will definitely choose Dare to save herself!" Kate finished. "Excellent!"

Patti looked modest. "Then all we have to do is dare her to go two doors down and knock on the Kinkaids' door."

"And hopefully Ginger will answer it," I said. This was a great plan! Ginger would be cornered at last!

"Christy's bound to ask where Ginger is the second she steps through the front door," Lauren pointed out as seven-thirty rolled around. We were checking out the Beekmans' leftovers because Lauren was hungry, as usual. Dr. Beekman is a fabulous cook.

"It will be okay," Kate said. "We'll stall her, like we planned, and make sure Mom is holed up in the basement with her latest project."

"I think that's a car in the driveway now," Patti said.

It was Christy, sure enough, and the first thing she said, after hello, was "Is Ginger here yet?"

"She will be soon," Kate said. "Take off your jacket and come into the kitchen. We've got blue-corn chips and Patti's Alaska dip. It has tuna and cream cheese and chili sauce and other good stuff in it."

"And we've got butterscotch popcorn," Lauren stuck in.

"Plus, Kate's super-fudge," I said.

"Fudge? I don't know . . . is that good for your — " Christy started up. No wonder she and Ginger got along so well!

But Kate said, "Let's *live* a little."

We piled everything on trays and carried them upstairs to Kate's bedroom. Dr. Beekman was at the hospital that night. Kate's little sister, Melissa, was spending the night at a friend's. Mrs. Beekman was busy in the basement, refinishing a table. So we pretty much had the whole house to ourselves.

Kate had borrowed her parents' portable TV. She switched it on to the "Top-Twenty Countdown" on *Video Trax*. We'd only gotten to Number Seventeen on the Hits List — the B29s singing, "You Are What You Were" — when Christy asked about Ginger again.

"Shouldn't she be here by now? Maybe we ought to call her house," Christy said.

"Hair," Kate mouthed at me.

"She's probably on her way," I said. "Christy, could you show us how you fix your hair in those great-looking" — I thought I heard Lauren moan softly at this point — "side-ponytails?"

"Sure!" Christy said. "The trick is to start out with lots of tight curls. Do you guys have curling irons and blow dryers?"

"We sure do," I said. We had come prepared.

"Great!" Christy said. "We have to wet our hair down . . ."

Talk about major frizzies! By the time we got back down the hall to Kate's room from the bathroom, my head looked like a mound of curly spaghetti!

But Christy is *good*. That night she managed to whip even *my* hair into shape. When she'd finished with us, there we sat, five side-ponytails in a row. I couldn't help smirking as I looked over at Kate. Poor Kate! She has the shortest hair of any of us, and her side-ponytail was more like a "side-explosion." But anything for a good cause, right?

Christy allowed herself a couple of seconds to gaze approvingly at her masterpieces. Then she said, "How late is it now? Maybe Ginger's not — "

"What about a quick game of Truth or Dare?" Kate said smoothly.

"That would be fun!" Patti said. "What about it, Christy?"

"Well, I'm sort of worried that — "

"Ginger can play, too, when she gets here," I said.

"Okay . . ." Christy agreed unenthusiastically.

Normally, we wouldn't even *start* a game of Truth or Dare so early in the evening. I mean, Truth or Dare can get pretty exciting, especially when it's almost midnight, and you have to sneak out of the house on a dare to tap on Donald Foster's window or something!

But that night. . . .

"Stephanie: Truth or Dare?" Kate said.

"Truth," I said.

Totally embarrassing, Patti had said earlier. Of course, the Truth I chose was something that Kate, Patti, and Lauren had already heard a bunch of times. But Christy hadn't, and it sounded *plenty* embarrassing to her.

I went on and on about the first boy I ever kissed — this complete dork named Gary Mims, at my elementary school back in the city. And Kate talked about wetting her pants when Henry Larkin made her fall off the seesaw in first grade. And Lauren told about the time she was absolutely convinced a flying saucer had landed on her garage, and even called the police, when it was really her brother Roger fooling around with a lantern.

Then Lauren said, "Christy — Truth or Dare?"

I'm sure all four of us crossed our fingers — I know *I* did.

Christy didn't answer for what seemed like ages. I was afraid she was going to want to quit playing and start trying to call Ginger on the phone. But Christy finally answered: "Dare?" Whew! Home free!

"Okay," Lauren said. "I'd like you to . . . sneak over to Eleven Pine Street, knock on the front door, and say hi to the new people who've just moved in!"

"Wha-at?" Christy said. "I can't do that! I don't even know them! And what about your mother, Kate?"

"Oh, she's in the basement," Kate said breezily.

"And if you don't know the people, what difference does it make if you knock on their door?" Patti pointed out sensibly. "You'll never have to see them again."

"How am I supposed to get to Eleven Pine Street without somebody spotting me?" Christy argued. "My parents would kill me if they found out I was wandering around after dark!"

"How would they ever find out? And it's only two houses down," Lauren said.

And Kate added, "We'll go with you most of the way, Christy."

"You chose Dare, Christy," I said. "Nobody ever goes back on a Dare."

Christy gave me a dirty look. "This is a dumb game!" But then she said crossly, "Oh, all right — let's get it over with!"

We slipped into our jackets, crept down the stairs — Kate put her finger to her lips, and pointed downward, toward the basement. We could hear Mrs. Beekman down there, using the electric sander.

The five of us tiptoed across the kitchen, Kate eased up the lock on the back door, and we stepped out onto the back porch.

"So far, so good!" she whispered. "Now — straight across the yard, Christy!"

Luckily, there was a moon out that night, so Christy didn't stumble over too many things. We made it across the Fosters' backyard, too, with no problems, even though practically every light in their house was blazing.

"I just hope Donald's watching the basketball game on TV, and not staring out his window," Lauren murmured to me as we pushed into the far hedge.

"And that Ginger's not standing near her living-room window, so that Christy spots her," I whispered back. We were counting on total surprise to make them start talking.

The Kinkaid living room was empty for the moment!

"This will be easy," Kate said to Christy. "Just run across this little strip of lawn, knock on the front door, say hi, and run back. We'll wait right here for you."

"Okay, okay," Christy grumbled.

She crawled out of the hedge and brushed off her beaded denim jacket — the one that matches Ginger's jacket from Just Juniors. Then she squared her shoulders and marched across the lawn.

The Kinkaids' front porch was dark. A few seconds after Christy had knocked, though, the porch light flicked on.

"Excellent," Patti murmured. "Now, if only it's Ginger who opens the door . . ."

We could hear somebody unlocking the wooden door on the inside. Then a voice yelled, "Christy! What are *you* doing here?"

"Ginger!" Christy exclaimed. "What are *you* doing here? This isn't your house!"

"Oh, Christy!" Ginger said, starting to cry. She pushed open the screen door, stepped out onto the porch, and gave Christy a big hug. "It's been *so* horrible. . . ."

"Good work, guys," I said for all four of us in

113

the hedge. "Let's go finish that fudge."

We were crossing the Fosters' backyard again when a window flew open and a blond head appeared. A boy's voice drawled, "So what is this? Parade of the Matching Munchkins?"

Our awful side-ponytails! Lauren and I got the giggles.

"Sssh, Donald — please!" Kate pleaded as we shot across his yard into her hedge.

Then we raced across Kate's yard, up the back steps, and into her kitchen. "That's that," she panted, locking the back door. "End of chapter. Case closed on Ginger Kinkaid."

We weren't surprised when the Beekmans' telephone rang about five minutes later. Kate grabbed it on the second ring. "Hello . . . yes . . . okay . . . sure . . . our pleasure." Then she hung up the phone, looking kind of smug.

"That was Ginger," Kate told us. "She and Christy are going to spend the night over at Christy's house. . . . And Ginger says thanks. She's going to drop over in a minute and pick up Christy's stuff. I told her we'd have it ready for her."

"We will indeed!" I whooped.

"Fabulous!" Patti said. "Now we can settle down to a normal Friday-night sleepover!"

"We can once this side-ponytail is history!" Lau-

114

ren said through gritted teeth. She jerked the elastic band off her head and flipped it into Kate's trash can.

"How about some fudge?" I suggested. "Then let's play Truth or Dare again, so I can dare Kate to call up a certain Mr. Taylor Sprouse. . . ."

"Oh, Stephanie!" Kate growled.

But then all four of us giggled. We had done it, we'd actually pulled it off! The Sleepover Friends are unstoppable!

Chapter
11

The next morning, after our memorable sleep-over, Kate, Patti, and I rode over to Lauren's to help the Hunters fix up their house on Brio Drive. Mr. Hunter was working on the hole in the living-room floor. Mrs. Hunter was scraping wallpaper off the walls in the front hall. And Roger was doing something to his room over the garage.

The four of us were painting the walls of the den peach, with pale gray trim — it's really a back bedroom on the second floor. As you can imagine, we were all dressed up in the crummiest clothes we could find — I was glad Ginger and Christy couldn't see us! I had on my mom's old baseball cap from her college team (at least it's *red*), a black T-shirt of Dad's that's coming apart at the seams, and torn jeans. Patti was wearing one of those white laboratory smocks from the Quarks, and a sailor's hat with the brim down, so she looked like some kind of crazy doctor on the high seas. Kate's always neat, but even she was wearing an oversized button-down shirt of her dad's, with sleeves that hung to her knees. Lauren had on her mom's gardening overalls, and a big blob of gray paint decorated her cheek.

We'd finished two walls and were starting to work on a third with our rollers and peach paint, when Roger yelled from the kitchen door, "Lauren! There's a lady in a truck here to see you!"

"A lady in a truck?" Lauren looked at us and shrugged her shoulders.

We put our paint rollers down and hurried downstairs to the kitchen. "Mrs. McWhinny!" Lauren exclaimed, opening the back door for her.

Alice McWhinny smiled apologetically. "Sorry to bother you on a Saturday, Lauren. Oh, hello, Stephanie — you're here, too. And your friends. Good. Maybe the young man can help us. . . ."

"Help us what, Mrs. McWhinny?" I said.

"I've brought Lauren's bed," Alice said, motioning over her shoulder toward the driveway.

There in the back of the small brown truck was the white iron bed, its brass knobs gleaming proudly.

"But Mrs. McWhinny! I've only paid . . ." — Lauren calculated — ". . . fourteen dollars on it. I still owe you . . . *eighty-six dollars!* And tax!'' she pointed out.

"Oh . . . well. Why not enjoy it in the meantime," Alice said vaguely. "I wanted to thank you, Lauren. . . ." Alice's thoughts wandered off in a slightly different direction for a second or two.

"Thank me?" Lauren prompted her.

"Yes. Yes. That money you found on Thursday . . . it had caused a terrible misunderstanding between Bernice Flanders from Bernice's Basement, and me."

Lauren and I nodded at each other — just as we'd thought!

"I'd sold a valuable piece of furniture for her, and I was *sure* I'd given her the money for it. I guess I had stuck it behind that vase instead, for safekeeping. . . ." Alice's voice trailed off. Then she added brightly, "But it's all been cleared up now, thanks to you. Bernice and I will be closing both stores for a week or so, and knocking down some walls, and rearranging. Then we'll reopen as Alice McWhinny/ Bernice Flanders Furniture Bargains again! Isn't that wonderful?!"

Alice must have noticed the weird expressions on Lauren's and my faces, because she quickly added, "Oh, I'll definitely want you to keep your jobs! We'll need you to help organize us. And Ber-

118

nice has a girl helping her out, too!"

What was it Kate had said at the sleepover the night before? "End of chapter. Case closed on Ginger Kinkaid"?

"Good-bye, Alice's Attic. Hello, Alice Mc-Whinny/Bernice Flanders Furniture Bargains," Lauren murmured forlornly. "And hello, Ginger Kinkaid!"

Roger and Mr. Hunter helped us set up Lauren's new bed in her room, although Kate insisted on cleaning it and polishing it first. Trust Kate! We were all dying to see what it looked like.

It looked fabulous! After Mr. Hunter put it together, and moved it between the two windows as I had done in my sketch, we all agreed that it looked totally hot!

"I'm going to sleep on it tonight!" Lauren said happily. "I can't wait!"

"What are you going to sleep *on*, Lauren?" Roger asked.

"Why, on . . ." Lauren started to point to the bed. "Oh," she said. She looked over at the three of us. "I don't have a *mattress*!" she said mournfully. The Sleepover Friends looked at each other, and at Lauren's sad face, and we couldn't help it. We burst out laughing. Lauren stared at us for a minute, then she started laughing, too. "What a plan!" she gasped between laughs. "I got the bed, all right, but I didn't think about a mattress!"

"Or a box spring," Patti giggled.

"Or sheets!" I was doubled over on the floor by this time.

"I know," Lauren said. "I'll get my sleeping bag and put it on the floor inside the bed frame!" We were all howling at the picture of Lauren sleeping on the floor, surrounded by her empty bedframe.

Mrs. Hunter came in.

"Oh, it's beautiful, Lauren," she said. "I can certainly see why you wanted it so badly. It goes perfectly in your new room." Then she noticed that we were all cracking up. She smiled.

"What's so funny?" she asked.

"Yeah, it *is* nice, Mom," Lauren said, grinning. "Too bad I don't have a mattress for it!"

Mrs. Hunter smiled widely. "Oh, my goodness, I didn't think of that either. Hmmm, let me see. We should be able to come up with something." She knitted her brow.

Lauren looked at her expectantly. I raised my eyebrows at Patti and Kate. What was Mrs. Hunter going to do?

"Well, I know," said Lauren's mother. "Your dad and I have been talking about getting a new mattress for *our* bed. I guess we can afford it right now. We'll give you our old mattress and box spring, until we can buy you a new one, too."

"Yay!" Lauren jumped up and down. We all hugged each other. Next week's sleepover was going to be better than ever!

"But Mrs. Hunter," I said. I can't help it — I always think of these things. "Won't Lauren need new sheets, too?" I was thinking that solid red ones go with almost everything. . . .

Lauren looked at her mother hopefully. Mrs. Hunter relented.

"Okay. Since you worked so hard to get your bed, we'll spring for one set of new sheets for it."

"Thanks, Mom!" Lauren yelled and hugged her mother. She looked over at us three. "What are you waiting for?" she yelled. "We have to change out of these yucky clothes and get over to the mall right away!"

"Hooray!" we all yelled. Sleepover Friends forever!

#32 A Valentine for Patti

"You could make Wayne Miller a valentine that says 'Get lost,' and sign it, 'Your Secret Un-Admirer,' " Stephanie sputtered.

"Don't even say *valentine* and his name in the same sentence!" Lauren shrieked.

Listening to Lauren's reaction to Wayne liking her made me even more uneasy about giving Henry a valentine. Just thinking about it made my stomach start to hurt. What if he didn't like me the same way I liked him? It would definitely have to be a secret.

SLEEPOVER FRIENDS™

by Susan Saunders

Available wherever you buy books...or use this order form.

Scholastic Inc. P.O. Box 7502, 2931 E. McCarty Street, Jefferson City, MO 65102

Please send me the books I have checked above. I am enclosing $_____
(please add $2.00 to cover shipping and handling). Send check or money order—no cash or C.O.D.s please.

Name _____

Address _____

City_____ State/Zip _____

Please allow four to six weeks for delivery. Offer good in U.S.A. only. Sorry, mail orders are not available to residents of Canada. Prices subject to change.   SLE690